THE WORLD OF SNL! SATURDAY NIGHT LIVE

HAL SCHUSTER

with Scott Nance and Kurt Fherenbach

Books for the entertainment buyer
PIONEER

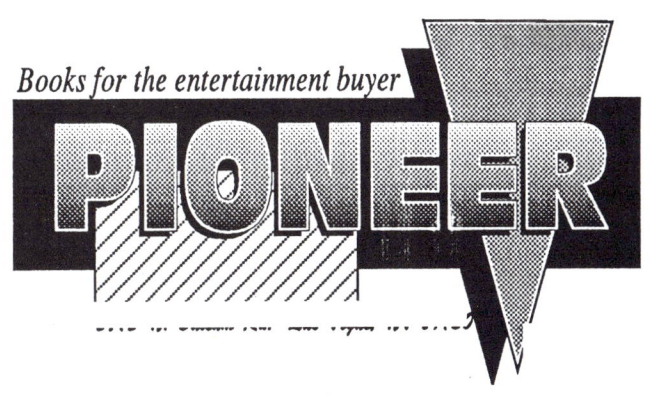

Library of Congress Cataloging-in-Publication Data
Hal Schuster, 1955—
    SNL! The World of Saturday Night Live

  1.   SNL! The World of Saturday Night Live (popular culture)
 I. Title

Copyright © 1992 by Pioneer Books, Inc. All rights reserved.
All artwork copyright © 1992 Pioneer Books, Inc. All photos are used to illustrate reviews only and are in no way intended to infringe on characters or concepts of any party. All rights reserved.

Published by Pioneer Books, Inc., 5715 N. Balsam Rd., Las Vegas, NV, 89130.

First Printing, 1992

Dedicated to that impulse that allows us to laugh in the face of tragedy.

HAL SCHUSTER writes about social and cultural trends. He is a frequent public speaker and active in arts, charitable and religious organizations. Previous books include Elvis!: The Magic Lives On and HOW TO USE A COMPUTER IN YOUR HOME OFFICE. He is listed in WHO'S WHO IN THE WORLD and frequently quoted by national publications. He is an active weight lifter and enjoys just about all sports. Schuster resides in Las Vegas.

7 The Show—
- 9   The Kids Come Out To Play
- 17   Getting Ready For Prime Time
- 23   Bringin Greenwich To Studio 8h
- 27   The Duel For Saturday Night
- 31   The Coming Of The Wolverines
- 39   The Show From Hell
- 47   Winning Awards From The Establishment
- 53   Fighting The Legions Of Decency
- 57   Now It Would Be Saturday Night Live
- 65   The Blues Brothers
- 69   From Underground To Beautiful People
- 77   The Love Children All Found Agents
- 83   Lorne Michaels Ends His Reign
- 91   Not Ready For Any Time
- 101   A Corporate Viking Funeral
- 109   The Future Of Saturday Night Live

117 The Players—
- 118   Dan Aykroyd
- 119   James Belushi
- 120   John Belushi
- 121   Chevy Chase
- 122   Billy Crystal
- 123   Jane Curtin
- 124   Joan Cusack
- 125   Denny Dillon
- 126   Robert Downey, Jr.
- 127   Julia Louis-dreyfus
- 128   Mary Gross
- 129   Anthony Michael Hall
- 130   Rich Hall
- 131   Jan Hooks
- 132   Tim Kazurinsky
- 133   Jon Lovitz
- 134   Dennis Miller
- 135   Eddie Murphy
- 136   Bill Murray
- 137   Lorraine Newman
- 138   Gilda Radner
- 139   Martin Short
- 140   Pamela Stephenson
- 141   Terry Sweeney

143 The Comedy—
- 145   Selected Sketches
- 157   The Lexicon

THE SHOW

THE KIDS COME OUT TO PLAY

It began with this:

"Good evening," said the first performer, Michael O'Donoghue.

"Good evening," echoed the second performer, in a thick Eastern European accent. The name of the second performer was John Belushi.

After this is repeated a bit, O'Donoghue checks his watch and says, "Let us begin. Repeat after me: I would like."

"I would like," parroted Belushi in the same accent.

"To feed your fingertips."

"To feed your fingertips."

"To the wolverines."

"To the wolverines!"

"Next, I am afraid we are out of badgers," continued O'Donoghue, and Belushi repeated. "Would you accept a badger in its place?"

"Hey, Ned exclaimed, let's boil the wolverines."

With that, the two performers fell to the ground, and *Saturday Night* was born.

That entire exchange—actually the entire ninety minute show—was broadcast live from New York City. No Hollywood doctoring.

It was guerrilla television late on Saturday nights. It was designed by its creator to be hip, irreverent, and to bring the baby-boomers, the "television generation" back to television. *Saturday Night* went to the throat of the Establishment. After this new show established itself, *Rolling Stone* said, "Not only have thirty million people tailored their weekend socializing to fit the show's 11:30 to 1:00 schedule, but their perception of what television can be as well."

The mastermind behind the night

The mastermind behind *Saturday Night* is a Canadian television writer and producer by the name of Lorne Michaels. It was Michaels' intention to make it appear the network closed for Saturday night and these kids came into the studio to play.

Michaels was first hooked on show business as a camp counselor, helping the kids put on productions of *Bye, Bye, Birdie* and *The Fantastiks* "He always seemed older than he was," said one friend, "and he always acted like he'd done something before even if he hadn't."

Michaels attended University College in Toronto, where he helped put on the *UC Follies* in 1964. The songs and skits looked a lot like those that would eventually appear on *Saturday Night*.

Bringing down the government with stand-up

During this production, Michaels met Hart Pomerantz, a former law student. The two developed a stand-up routine; Michaels played Pomerantz's straight man.

SNL! THE STORY OF SATURDAY NIGHT LIVE

They got enough attention in Canada that the Canadian Broadcasting Corporation offered them jobs as comedy writers for the radio show *Five Nights a Week at This Time*. Amidst success, Michaels' maverick streak began to show. He wanted to "bring down the government" with his comedy, he later remembered wistfully.

The Lorne and Hart team would eventually leave over differences with the government-controlled network.

In the States and on the air

They got jobs as junior writers on NBC's *The Beautiful Phyllis Diller Show*. The material was less than stellar and NBC axed the series after only nine weeks.

The duo tried again, this time for *Laugh-In*. The material was better, but the head writer rejected all their jokes about Richard Nixon. Rewritten almost unto death, Michaels and Pomerantz still got the satisfaction of seeing hints of their ideas on the air.

They also started sending jokes to Woody Allen. Allen never used their material.

Back in Canada for their own specials

Michaels and Pomerantz resolved their disputes with Canadian Broadcasting when the network offered them their own series of comedy specials. They did four a year under different names: *The Hart and Lorne Terrific Hour* and *Today Makes Me Nervous*.

The specials were another step toward *Saturday Night*. Michaels and Pomerantz served as hosts, supported by a repertory company and musical guests such as Cat Stevens and James Taylor. One occasional comedic guest was a fellow Canadian, Dan Aykroyd.

Michaels learns comedy

Michaels developed his comedy-sense under two disparate influences: the Golden Age of TV and the Sixties underground subculture.

The flower-child acid influence was obvious. One of Michaels' friends remarked, "It was always the Beatles, acid, and mushrooms."

Michaels also watched TV constantly. One story has it that Michaels watched so much television that when he moved from the second to the seventh floor of his building, he had to be carried during a commercial.

He was fanatical over *The Tonight Show* and *The Honeymooners*. His comedy was rounded out by *Monty Python's Flying Circus* which began to run in Canada in 1970. "It was miraculous to me, a revelation," Michaels later said of the British comedy.

Saturday night almost arrives

Tensions flared between Lorne and Hart. Michaels was tired of being the straight man.

They parted in 1972, and Michaels headed for Hollywood on his own. Michaels hired Sandy Wernick as his agent.

Wernick pitched Michaels' idea for a youth-oriented comedy series to NBC. NBC executive Larry White bit, and Michaels screened some samples.

Although White thought it was hilarious, he said, "No one will understand what you're doing!"—and the project died. *Saturday Night* would wait three more years while Michaels produced specials for Lily Tomlin.

SNL! THE STORY OF SATURDAY NIGHT LIVE

Late night programming wars

Saturday Night came another step closer when Lorne Michaels met Dick Ebersol.

In the '70s, Johnny Carson's *Tonight Show* was already a winner in weekday late-night programming for NBC. On weekends the network broadcast Carson re-runs. Many affiliates balked, skipping the repeats and broadcasting their own programming, usually old movies.

The weekend *Tonight* ratings were so bad NBC advertising people gave away the spots as a bonus for their clients. Carson was embarrassed by the poor weekend ratings and wanted it fixed.

Dick Ebersol wasn't the typical network exec. He seemed more at home with the hippie set—long hair and all—than in a studio office.

His suit was decidedly corporate. As NBC's new director of late-night weekend programming, it was his job to fix the Carson mess.

Ebersol wanted a variety show to replace the *Tonight* re-runs on Saturday nights. When Michaels' agent, Wernick, caught wind of the plan, he told Ebersol, "Dick, there's only one guy you should meet."

After five thousand years of civilization, Saturday night finally arrives

They met. In May of '75 Ebersol pitched *Saturday Night* to an NBC affiliates' gathering. He pledged that the new show would be top-notch, with guests "such as" Lily Tomlin, Richard Pryor, and George Carlin, and musical acts "such as" the Rolling Stones and Stevie Wonder. He added that the show would feature a company of comedy players from cities "such as" New York and Los Angeles.

Ebersol's "such as"'s were important. No guests—comedic or musical—had been approached; no comedy players yet auditioned.

Ebersol's presentation attracted interest. Even the King of the Night, Johnny Carson, wanted to know more.

The meeting between Carson and Ebersol and Michaels was a foretaste of the all-out assault against the Establishment *SNL* would become. Carson epitomized that Establishment.

Getting the royal nod from the King of Latenight

"So," the King of Latenight said, "you guys are only going to be on one night a week?"

Once Michaels and Ebersol got comfortable, Carson continued, "I've heard about your show, and I think we've really got to talk about it. It's got similarities to mine."

The young men quickly emphasized the differences. "What we really have is a comedy-variety show," insisted Ebersol.

"Well, we have variety here, too," Carson countered.

"Our show will be mostly sketches," Ebersol replied.

"You mean there's going to be no talk or interviews?" Carson asked.

"None at all," was the answer.

Carson's producer, Fred de Cordova, entered to join the conversation. Carson invited the newcomer to express his concerns. De Cordova wondered about music conflicts. Michaels and Ebersol said that they would only feature rock. "Oh, there's no problem there, then," de Cordova said. "That's not our kind of music."

They shook hands and Michaels and Ebersol left. Unsaid, but universally understood, was the main difference between *Tonight* and *Saturday Night*. *Tonight* was aimed at the parents of the youth who would watch *Saturday Night*.

After the meeting with Carson, NBC executive Dave Tebet called Ebersol. "They liked you. They thought you were fine boys," he said. When he saw the final product, Carson would change his mind.

GETTING READY FOR PRIME TIME

II

There had been a lot of nay-sayers at NBC as far as *Saturday Night* went. One executive complained, "This show is a high risk from a research standpoint, because I don't believe you get enough 18 to 24 (year olds) to stay home on Saturday nights to watch this show."

The suits suggested Michaels get Rich Little to host a show, and Bob Hope, yeah Bob Hope. They thought the University of Southern California marching band might make a wonderful musical guest.

The execs were a little taken aback when Michaels instead announced he wanted Richard Pryor as a host and the Rolling Stones as musical guests. Still, they figured anything would be better than the *Tonight* re-runs.

> *"There's something incredibly ballsy about getting up, live, before 20 or 30 million people every week and doing complex comedy,"* said one comedy writer not associated with Saturday Night. *"I remember watching the first show and being amazed at how sophisticated it was. I wasn't always laughing—for the first few programs I was just trying to get a handle on it—but there was no way to turn it off. For the first time in television comedy, it seemed to me that almost anything was possible."*

NBC president Herb Schlosser was convinced. "I want a live variety show from (studio) 8H, and these boys are going to give it to me," he announced, silencing all dissent.

Putting Saturday Night together from scratch

Saturday Night was becoming a reality. "I was absolutely convinced of the rightness of what I was doing," remembered Lorne Michaels.

Michaels went to work building his show. He wanted what he termed "enlightened amateurs", talent that wouldn't be stopped by television conventions.

Director Dave Wilson and Audrey Hickman were the only ones in the cast and crew with an extensive TV background. Michaels made it clear they weren't to impose conventions on the cast or show.

Schlosser believed in the show, but not too much. NBC gave Michaels a budget that could produce "a cross between the *Tonight Show* and *Meet the Press*."

Fortunately Michaels didn't need expensive established talent.

Co-opting the Comedy Underground for television

Lorne Michaels found his cast and crew in the "comedy underground". Like most artists on "the fringe", the radical comics weren't rich and *were* looking for work.

Michaels frequented comedy clubs recruiting the best and the brightest. First to be hired was the late Gilda Radner, whom Michaels had known in Canada. He lured her from an impending deal with a syndicated show.

Many innovative comedians were wary of Michaels, seeing him as part of the entertainment Establishment. They didn't want to get sucked into another *Gilligan's Island*, the sort of mindless comedy they were rebelling against.

Michaels seemed sincere about his comedic revolution. He hired writers Michael O'Donoghue and Anne Beatts from the *National Lampoon*. O'Donoghue had written a piece for *Lampoon* called the "Vietnam Baby Book", in which he explained tips for new Vietnamese mothers on how to treat napalm wounds and that a Vietnamese baby's first word was "medic."

Beatts was no less biting. She once thought of having business cards printed that read: "Anne Beatts, Ball Buster."

Chevy Chase comes to Saturday Night

Another quick hire was a young comedian named Chevy Chase. Michaels met Chase in Los Angeles. He spotted him cracking jokes while waiting in line to see *Monty Python and the Holy Grail*.

Michaels offered him a job writing. Chase wanted to perform. Only after being fired from his job in summer stock did he accept Michaels' offer.

Other writers included Alan Zweibel, who moonlighted at a deli; Herb Sargent, who had been a writer for Steve Allen's original *Tonight* show in the Fifties; and the bizarre team of Al Franken and Tom Davis who had worked every year as Santa Claus and Winnie-the-Pooh for a department store.

Building the cast for Saturday Night

Garrett Morris was hired as a writer. He had become established as one of Harry Belafonte's backup singers. When he didn't work out as a writer, Michaels made him one of the original cast members.

Laraine Newman came in from Los Angeles. Another possible was a young radical comic named John Belushi. When he entered Michaels' office, Belushi repeated, "TV sucks!" several times. Michaels suggested he come back for the auditions.

Comedian Richard Belzer felt that having his friend John Belushi audition was like telling Michaeangelo, "Do this drawing and we'll see about the murals." Still, Belushi was eager.

The New York auditions rivaled the actual show for sheer entertainment. Every two-bit performer in the city showed up. Some were funny; some weren't. They weren't what the show was looking for.

One promising tryout was Jane Curtin, a member of The Proposition comedy troupe from Boston. She and a friend auditioned together presenting a sketch Curtin had written. It was about two housewives planning for the annual big tornado—"Can I borrow your centerpiece for the tornado this year?".

Bill Murray also gave it a try. He had developed his talent with the Second City company.

Between auditions, a young man ran on stage with an umbrella and a briefcase under each arm. He wore a derby, stood and shouted, "I've been waiting out there for three hours and I'm not going to wait anymore and I'm going to miss my plane! That's it, gentlemen, you've had your chance."

He walked off. That man was Dan Aykroyd. He didn't know he was already under consideration by Lorne and an audition wasn't necessary.

The Belushi audition

The cap to the audition event arrived when Belushi finally auditioned.

Like Aykroyd, Belushi was impatient. "What the fuck am I doing here?" he would ask himself out loud as he waited. "I hate television!"

Finally, Belushi was up. He auditioned in his samurai pool shark character, his hair pulled up in a knot. By the time he was done, a crowd had gathered to watch the temperamental genius.

Assembling the final opening cast

After the auditions ended, Michaels and his writing and production staff conferred on their final selections. Money was tight; only a few could be hired.

Dick Ebersol wanted Curtin to balance the already-hired Radner and Newman. Belushi was a favorite. The real choice was between Murray and Aykroyd. The latter won out.

The cast was assembled. They went to work on the premiere. "It's like musicians jamming," commented writer Herb Sargent about the *Saturday Night* cast and crew.

"See, it's comedy without the mask," Gilda Radner once explained. "It's based on honesty and ordinariness. I'm not hiding behind a funny nose and glasses or a big production. I'm saying, 'This is *me* and this is what's vulnerable about me.'"

III

BRINGING GREENWICH TO STUDIO 8H

It Was Good Enough for Toscanini...

Saturday Night debuted on October 11, 1975 in studio 8H of NBC's Rockefeller Center headquarters. The studio would become the show's permanent home.

Saturday Night followed many outstanding productions in 8H. NBC Radio broadcast a Christmas Day concert by the NBC Symphony conducted by 70-year-old Arturo Toscanini in 1937. The concerts continued for almost two decades.

The studio is the largest in New York with about 8,000 square feet. TV shows that have made their mark from the studio include *Your Hit Parade*, *The Texaco Huntley-Brinkley Report*, *What's My Line?*, and *Match Game*.

> *"Instead of all shiny and Mylar, it looked sort of run-down and beat-up, like New York City did,"* Michaels explained.

Something was bound to happen to that studio when Lorne Michaels and his radical comic troops took over. And something did happen.

Michaels loved the work set designer Eugene Lee conceived for the studio. Lee wanted to rip out the bleachers and replace them with swivel seats, and use oak and brick. It would create the atmosphere of a dark Greenwich Village cafe. "Instead of all shiny and Mylar, it looked sort of run-down and beat-up, like New York City did," Michaels explained.

Michaels and executive Ebersol took the mock-up model to the budget execs, who put the redesign at $250,000 and up—about three times more than NBC would allow.

Michaels felt 8H was woefully out-of-date. The suits quickly rejected the plan. One said, "If it was good enough for Toscanini, it's good enough for Lorne Michaels."

Insisting on revolution in 8H

Michaels had already developed a reputation for not giving up easily. It annoyed many execs and some NBC technical crew. Many of the crew had worked there since the Milton Berle era. "He always had an answer," said the stage manager of Michaels, "quick and off-handed, not friendly."

Michaels and Ebersol took their model and hopped an elevator to president Herb Schlosser's suite. Their fast talking convinced the boss.

He issued a memo regarding the large pricetag of Michaels' new 8H: "Please be advised that management is aware and it is to be treated as an explainable overage."

After the remake, 8H could seat 300 for *Saturday Night*'s live studio audience. The three original sets were replaced with eight new ones.

Two of the new sets are permanent. The center set—called "home base"— is where the weekly guest host delivers their monologue. Stage-right is where the musical guests perform. The others change week to week.

SNL! THE STORY OF SATURDAY NIGHT LIVE 25

Five hundred lights illuminate the studio, supported by 30 tons of steel. Without the special air-conditioning, under those lights, 8H would cook at 140 degrees Fahrenheit.

Ready to roll for Saturday night

Michaels now had a staff, a cast, and a place to call home. NBC had invested over a quarter of a million dollars in the show. It would very hard to turn back.

IV

THE DUEL FOR SATURDAY NIGHT

Saturday Night Live was originally titled *NBC's Saturday Night. Saturday Night Live* was Michaels' original choice, but it had already been taken by the competition.

ABC had the same idea as NBC. They wanted to grab the youth market. It was planned as a vehicle for Howard Cosell to lift himself out of the limits of sports broadcasting. The network called it's show *Saturday Night Live With Howard Cosell*.

The Saturday Nights compete for talent

Each *Saturday Night* was conscious of the other. Cosell's show hired Don Mischer, Michaels' first choice for director.

ABC's series was interested in Gilda Radner and Jane Curtin, but felt John Belushi was too uncontrolled

> *The Bay City Rollers, an inoffensive Scottish mainstream pop band, was the featured musical guest. A far cry from the Sex Pistols, the British punk band Michaels wanted.*

when he auditioned. Bill Murray, who Michaels passed over for Aykroyd, found a job with Cosell. So did future NBC *Saturday Night* player Christopher Guest.

27

Both shows mixed music and sketches and a host. There the similarities ended.

ABC called their repertory company the "Ready for Prime Time Players", but the company had little to do. There was none of the raw theatrical element Michaels envisioned. Cosell and his execs wanted "high-tech" with acts beamed in via satellite.

Cosell's not cool after all

ABC's venture debuted three weeks before NBC's. Michaels' writing team of Al Franken and Tom Davis held a party for the auspicious occasion.

There were gales of laughter from Michaels' people; not with Cosell's show, *at* it. The Bay City Rollers, an inoffensive Scottish mainstream pop band, was the featured musical guest. A far cry from the Sex Pistols, the British punk band Michaels wanted.

The humor tried to be hip, but played too safe; too constrained within limits.

When it came time to name the players on the NBC *Saturday Night*, they mocked Cosell's show. If his cast was "Ready for Prime Time" Michaels' cast would be the "Not-Ready for Prime Time" players.

SNL! THE STORY OF SATURDAY NIGHT LIVE   29

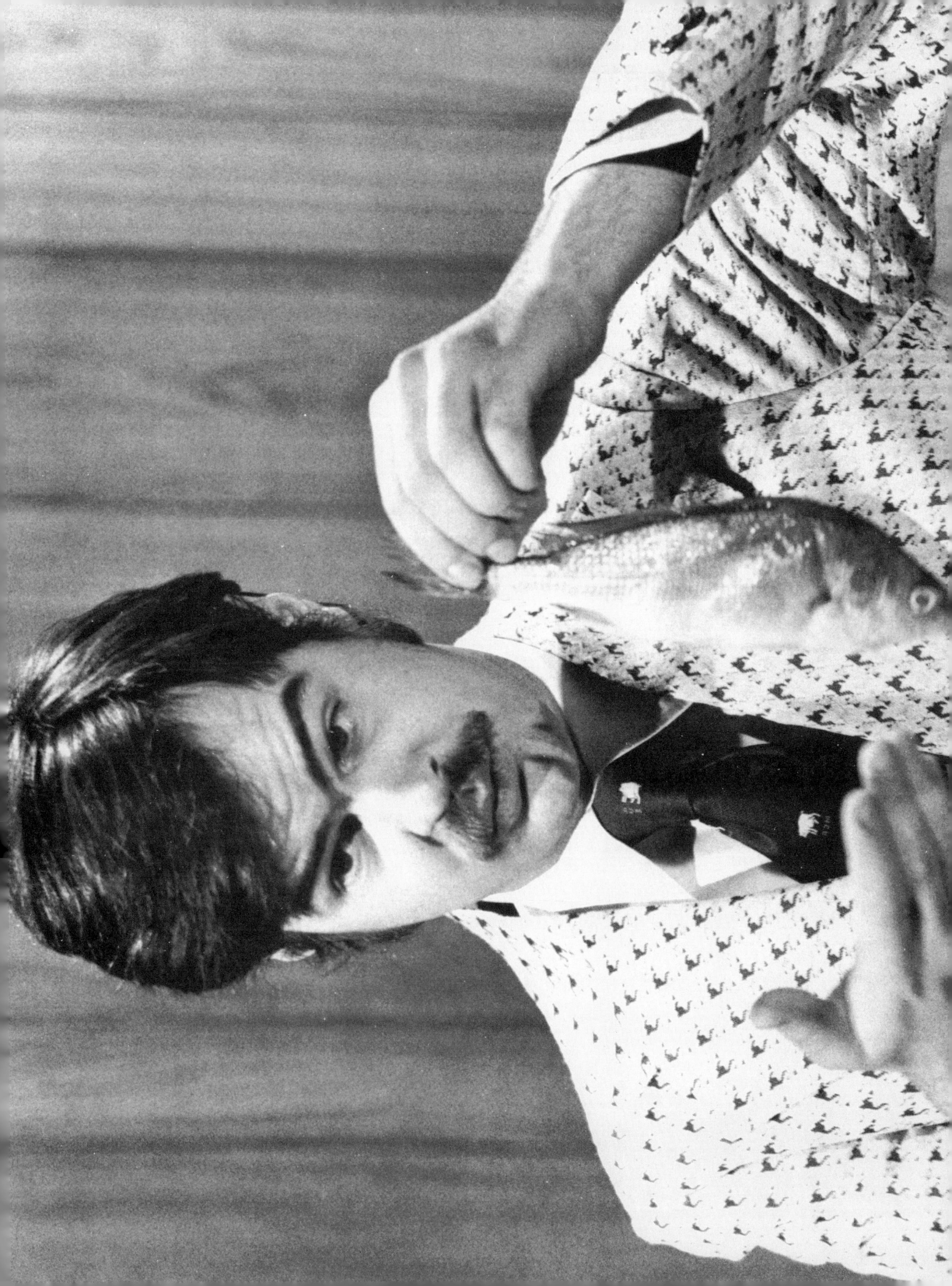

V THE COMING OF THE WOLVERINES

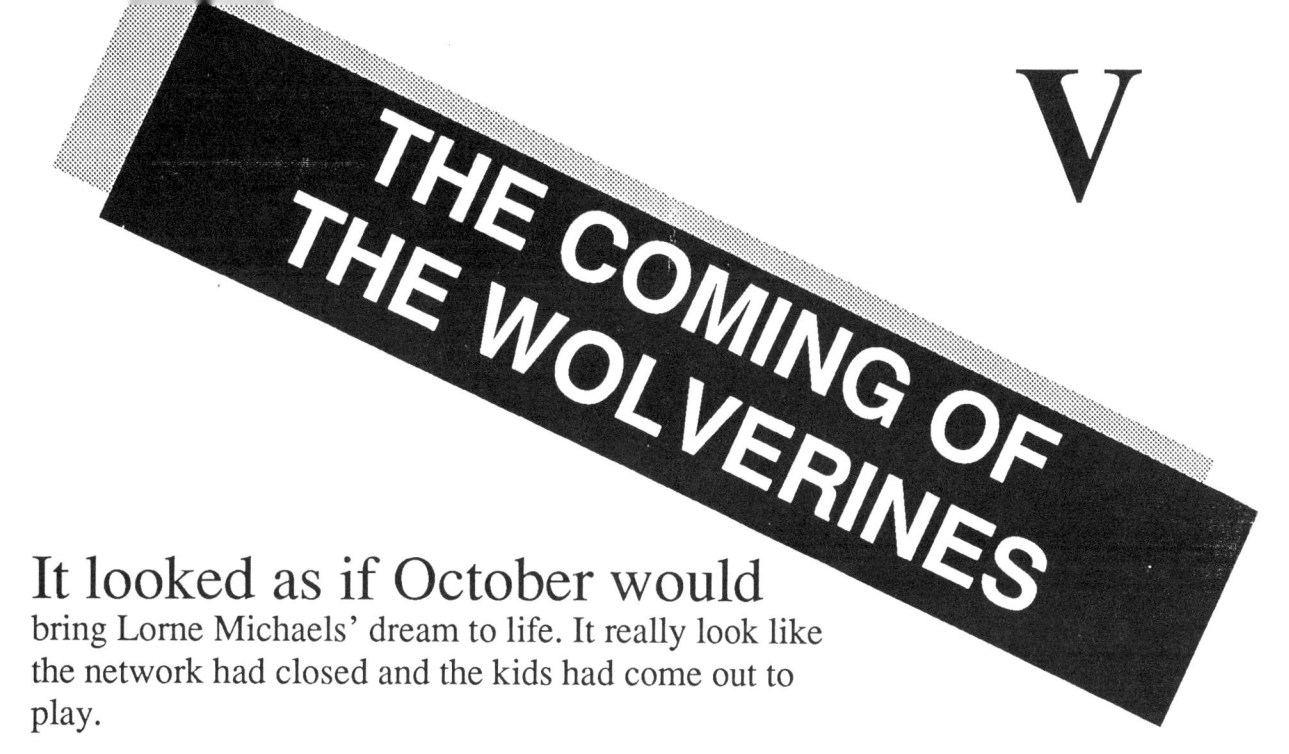

It looked as if October would bring Lorne Michaels' dream to life. It really look like the network had closed and the kids had come out to play.

They started with a "cold opening" showing none of the normal credits or announcements at the beginning of the show. Instead O'Donoghue and Belushi presented the first sketch, "The Wolverines". It came off beautifully. The audience was bewildered.

> *John Belushi told Rolling Stone, "What we are, man, is actors. And this show's good when we're working together, all of us, in a sketch as comic actors, playing off each other, with each other, not reading cue cards."*

Lorne Michaels had always said he knew the right ingredients, but not the correct measures of each. They would experiment on the air. The right mix would grow organically.

Michaels promised the network he'd find it by the 10th show. NBC president Herb Schlosser said that would be the show he'd watch.

Confusing the audience

True to his prediction, the proportions were off for the premiere. George Carlin hosted. The company of players failed to provide focus.

Chevy Chase presented a parody newscast, "Weekend Update", for three minutes. The sketch later became a *Saturday Night* hallmark. In the beginning, it confused audiences.

Many thought Chase was the star of the show. Actually Chase came aboard as a writer and wasn't even paid as part of the repertory.

Interesting bits on the air waves

The first *Saturday Night* didn't quite fail, though. Dan Ackroyd provided a beautiful bit about two home security salesmen. They break into a home, menace the parents, and kidnap the kids to prove the family needs a home security system.

"In the event of a radioactive firestorm," Ackroyd demanded, "how secure are your foodstuffs?"

The late Andy Kaufman (Latka on *Taxi*) startled the audience by singing the *Mighty Mouse* theme song: "Here I come to save the day!"

Chase's Weekend Update got laughs. He revealed then-President Gerald Ford's campaign slogan: "If he's so dumb, how come he's President?"

Carlin's closing monologue was irreverent. He called God only a "semisupreme being" because "everything he ever made died." NBC's Dave Tebet was mortified. He thought, their switchboard had lit up with calls offended by that remark.

On target, but missing the mark

Offensive or not, *Saturday Night* got people, if fewer than hoped, to sit up and take notice of a different voice. It inspired an emerging comedian named Steve Martin.

Although some complained he wanted to steal the show, Chase proved he understood comedy. He called it comedy that goes "through the lens and right into the viewer's lap."

For all its innovation, *Saturday Night* was not an instant hit. The debut scraped up a 23 share. Successful prime time shows earn a 30.

It didn't get popular acceptance or the support of the critical community. John O'Connor of the New York *Times* wrote: "It's not enough for the new *Saturday Night* concept to be transmitted live. Even an offbeat showcase needs quality, an ingredient conspicuously absent from the dreadfully uneven comedy efforts of the new series."

The second time around

Michaels missed with the second show, too. His mix still wasn't right. It was essentially a music special.

His friend Paul Simon agreed to host a show featuring his reunion with former partner Art Garfunkel. The writers were pleased. They were exhausted after the premiere and let Simon's music fill the time.

The actors felt shortchanged. Again, they went almost unseen. They felt relegated to the status ABC's Ready for Time Players suffered amidst the Bay City Rollers and Howard Cosell.

Closer to the mark

The actors emerged in the third show. It too had problems.

Rob Reiner, then "Meathead" on Norman Lear's *All In The Family*, hosted. He insisted on performing a sketch in which he played a Vegas lounge lizard singer. It wasn't funny.

Michaels tried to talk him out of it, but Reiner persisted. Michaels didn't feel secure enough for one of his tantrums, so he let it go. One writer called Michaels "sniveling and whining".

Chase went on and his Vegas bit bombed. With the host finally out of the main focus, the players took over.

Jane Curtin hosted a parody talk show, "Dangerous but Inept", in which Laraine Newman took the part of would-be presidential assassin Squeaky Fromme. Belushi impersonated blues singer Joe Cocker, but it was as a Bee that he brought the house down.

The coming of the bees

The Bees had been introduced in an earlier show when two were in a hospital. The mother had a baby, and the nurse proclaimed, "Congratulations, it's a drone."

Michaels liked dressing the players as Bees to get them together in a silly way. John Belushi, the rebel from the start, didn't like it. He told *Rolling Stone*, "What we are, man, is actors. And this show's good when we're working together, all of us, in a sketch as comic *actors*, playing off each other, *with* each other, *not* reading cue cards, like we have to, but memorizing the lines in advance, making eye contact, not dressing like fucking *bees*! You can*not* put an actor in a bee costume and say, 'Well, that funny dress will make up for the weak writing.' Sure, they'll laugh at the antennae once or twice, after that, forget it, it's repetitive shit. *I hate the fucking bees!*"

During the Reiner show, Belushi played a Bee waiter, serving Reiner and his wife, Penny Marshall. Breaking character, Reiner bellowed, "I was told 'no Bees' when I signed on to this. They're not helping the show—they're ruining the show."

Belushi responded, "I'm sorry if you think we're ruining your show, Mr. Reiner. But, see, you don't understand—we didn't ask to be Bees. You see, you've got Norman Lear and a first-rate writing staff. But this is all they came up with for us. *Do you think we like this?* No, no, Mr. Reiner, we don't have any choice."

The audience applauded thunderously.

Belushi continued, "You see, we're just like you were five years ago, Mr. Hollywood California Number One Show Big Shot! That's right—we're just a bunch of actors looking for a break, that's all! What do you *want* from us? Mr. Reiner, Mr. Star. What did you expect? *The Sting?*"

Still working on the mix with number four

The fourth show went better. It all seemed to fall into place.

Candice Bergen, the movie star who would later claim fame on *Murphy Brown*, hosted. She was the first honest-to-goodness movie star many of the cast worked with. Rather than take a superior air, she appeared honored to be with *them*.

At one point during writing and pre-production, Belushi came into Michaels' office while Michaels and Bergen were conferring. Belushi suggested he play film director

Sam Peckinpah and Bergen portray the actress he abused on the set.

To demonstrate, Belushi slammed Bergen against the wall, pummeled her with his fists, and threw her behind Michaels' desk where he promptly jumped on her. Michaels was horrified. Bergen giggled and laughed throughout the demonstration.

When the show went on, the players got as much exposure as Bergen. She won the company's admiration. At the end of the evening, they all joined her on stage and each presented her with a red rose. It was the first time the players joined the host at the end.

Winning critical acclaim—at last

The show that night had been delayed by NBC because of a long movie, and it hurt the ratings. The Bergen show only got a 16 share. Yet the critical support lacking the first few weeks turned around.

Tom Shales of the Washington *Post* commented, "*NBC's Saturday Night* can boast the freshest satire on commercial TV, but it is more than that. It is probably the first network series produced by and for the television generation—those late-war and post-war babies who were the first to have TV as a sitter. They loved it in the '50s, hated it in the '60s, and now they're trying to take it over in the '70s . . . ."

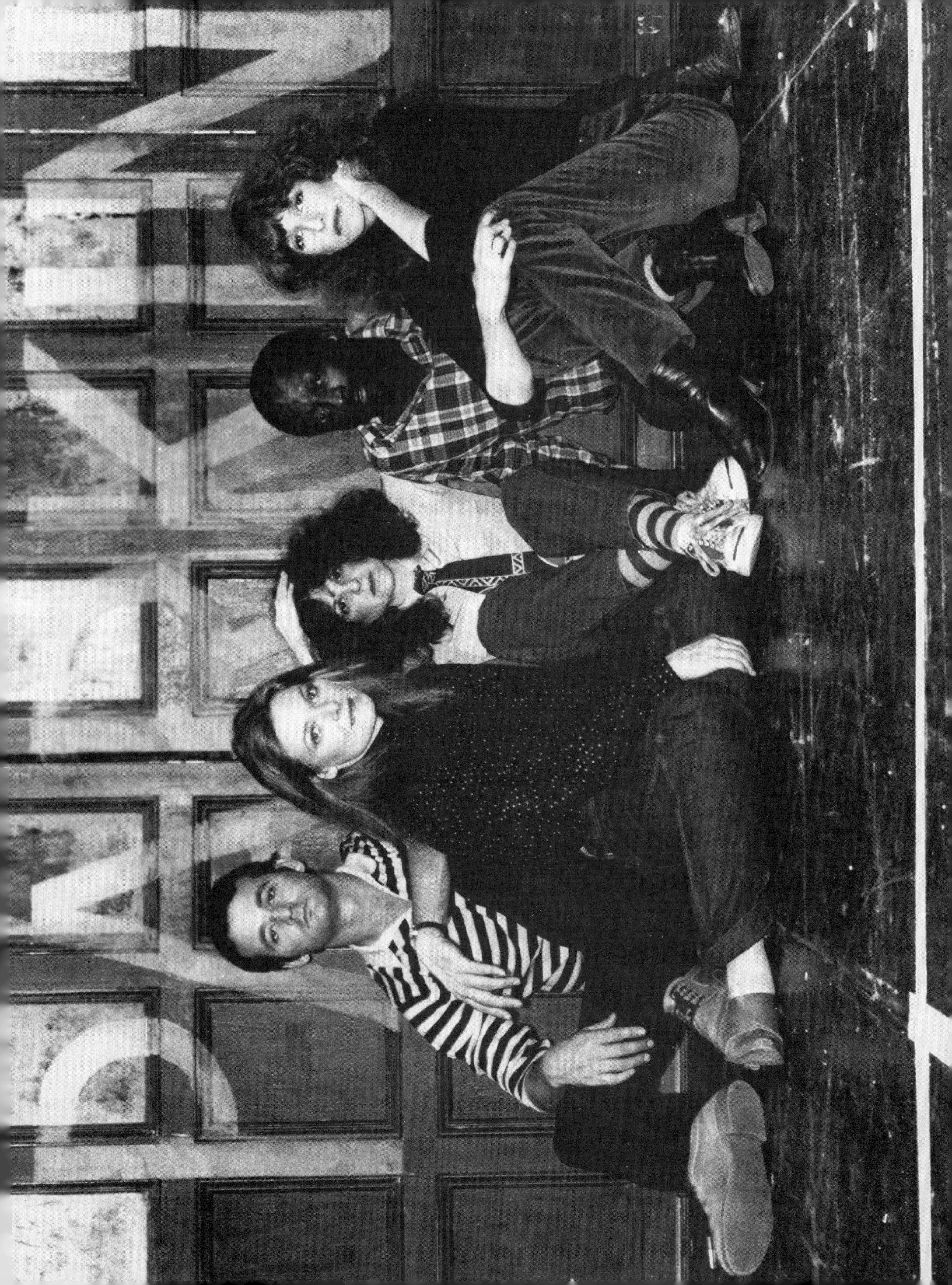

VI

THE SHOW FROM HELL

The *Saturday Night* cast and crew didn't care if they scored a ratings success. Or about O'Connor's scathing review.

Michaels posted it in the offices for all to laugh at. These were underground radicals. They weren't looking for Establishment approval.

The Bergen show was a climax of sorts. A successful Hollywood star shared *Saturday Night*'s unique vision on its own terms.

> *"I've watched your program prior to this and I've found your program to be unsettling and insulting and sadistic. I (my family too) will take no more of your abuse. You've gone too far . . . . I (my friends and family too) will tell others in our community of your Satanic show. You must all be demons."*

The following week wasn't very magical.

The two weeks following host Robert Klein could bring magic or disaster. Lily Tomlin hosted one week, Richard Pryor the next.

Lily Tomlin's Feminist show

Lorne Michaels had worked with Tomlin on her CBS specials and gave her utmost respect during her week. She was selective. She wanted nothing sexist, and wanted the women of the show to provide the focus for the week.

One sketch was a Feminist standout. It taught women to harass and leer at hunky construction workers as much as those construction workers harassed and leered at them.

Tomlin played the teacher. Belushi turned the part of the construction worker down flat. Aykroyd was convinced to take the part.

Tomlin taught pick-up lines to the women in the "class", including, "Hey, studmuffins, wanna make bouncy bouncy?"

Richard Pryor on Saturday night

Tomlin's show was calm and orderly compared to the chaos of Pryor.

To get Pryor, Michaels had to fight a war on two fronts. One with an NBC frightened Pryor was too wild, and a second with Pryor himself. The war with NBC was easier.

Both finally agreed with conditions. NBC insisted on a 5 second time delay to allow the censor to *bleep* vulgarity.

Pryor placed more complex conditions. His own entourage would join the *Saturday Night* repertory. He would bring in a black writer, Paul Mooney, a black actor, Thalmus Rasulala, and Gil Scott-Heron, a black musical guest. He insisted on including his white ex-wife, Shelley, in the show. (She did her own peculiar stand-up routine.)

Michaels agreed to all the conditions, but said Pryor "had better be funny."

When his show came, the regular cast noticed that several of Pryor's group carried guns. Writer Michael O'Donoghue was the first in trouble with Pryor. The writer suggested a sketch saying people shouldn't be judged on skin color, but on the size of their nostrils. Pryor picked up a whiskey bottle and threatened O'Donoghue.

The night of the show, Pryor brought a huge group of friends— and suddenly NBC security guards showed up. To satisfy the network, the time delay had been set up but kept top secret so as not to anger Pryor. Even the clocks in the studio were turned back five seconds so no one would notice the delay.

Pryor said "ass" twice on the air, but not a bleep came out of the censor. The profanity was edited from taped versions broadcast later to the Western time zone.

A winning performance

Pryor delivered a winning performance with the Not-Ready for Prime Time Players at his side. As always, the Weekend Update was a winner.

Radner did her editorializing old lady, Emily Litella. She was raving against the "busting" of schoolchildren. When Chase corrected her, saying the issue was really "busing" them, she responded with a winning "Oh...never mind."

Pryor and Chase performed the standout sketch, in which Chase was a job interviewer giving Pryor a "word association test" which quickly turned ugly.

"White," Chase said. "Black," Pryor replied.

"Negro." "Whitie."

"Tarbaby." "What'd you say?"

"Tarbaby." "Ofay."

"Colored." "Redneck!"

"Junglebunny." "Peckerwood!"

"Burrhead." "Cracker!"

"Spearchucker." "White trash!"

"Junglebunny." "Honkey."

"Spade!" "Honkey. Honkey."

"Nigger." "*Dead* honkey."

Of course, the skit had been worked out in advance with Pryor. The audience seemed anxious behind the laughter.

Candice Bergen, Lily Tomlin, and Richard Pryor proved *Saturday Night* had made it to the big leagues. They were *legitimate* radical video guerillas and began to satirize bigger subjects in even more off-beat ways.

Chevy Chase began to portray a bumbling President Ford.

Where no man had gone

In one memorable early sketch, Belushi played Captain Kirk of *Star Trek* as NBC canceled that show. The host that week, Elliot Gould, played the NBC exec who boarded the starship *Enterprise* to break the bad news.

The starship crew regard Gould's character as an alien. Spock (played by Ackroyd) attempts to knock him out with his "famous Vulcan nerve pinch", but nothing happens.

Gould mistakenly believes Spock is admiring his suit. "Isn't that fabric something? . . . Oh, Nimoy, we'll need the ears back, too, I'm afraid," Gould says, plucking off Spock's ear tips.

Rosebud by any other name

Saturday Night also aimed its comedic cross-hairs at the film classic, *Citizen Kane*. In the sketch, Aykroyd played Charles Foster Kane.

This time Kane's dying word isn't "Rosebud" but "roast beef." Kane had been trying to ask for a "roast beef on rye with mustard."

Inviting the Beatles to Saturday night

The biggest stunt didn't come in a sketch. Lorne Michaels appeared on the air to invite the Beatles to reunite on *Saturday Night*. He held up a check for $3,000 and said, "All you have to do is sing three Beatles songs. 'She loves you/yeah, yeah, yeah.' That's a thousand dollars right there. You know the words. It'll be easy.

"Like I said, this is made out to the Beatles—you divide it up any way you want. If you want to give Ringo less, it's up to you. I'd rather not get involved. I'm sincere about this. If this helps you reach a decision to reunite, it's well worth the investment. You have agents. You know where I can be reached. Just think about it, okay?"

A few weeks later, Michaels upped the ante to $3,200. He had no idea until later how close he had come to success. In an interview with *Playboy* shortly before his death, John Lennon said, "Paul and I were together watching that show. He was visiting us at our place at the Dakota. We were watching it and almost went down to the studio just as a gag. We nearly got into a cab, but we were actually too tired."

Defending his material

The show became more sure of itself. The network wasn't so sure. At that point in the '70s, network censors were the byword. Called "Standards editors", they would censor anything they deemed offensive.

From the beginning, Lorne Michaels pitted his aggressive style against the censors. He defended his writers' material, whether a sketch or just a single word. "Carson used that word on the 14th of October. Look it up," Michaels would say.

In some cases, Michaels appealed a censor's decision to higher and higher execs at NBC, conceding smaller jokes to keep the one he wanted. Sometimes a joke Michaels thought would be censored passed without question.

Don Pardo was to announce Weekend Update was sponsored by "Pussy Whip", the first dessert for cats. The censor thought it hilarious. Michaels quickly learned censors were much less likely to object to material they laughed at.

Some jokes went right over the censors' heads. One was another "ad" for Update: "Hershey Highway, turning America's taste around for 50 years." Evidently, the suits didn't understand the reference to anal sex.

In a few rare cases, the show ignored the censors. One such sketch involved Dan Ackroyd as a refrigerator repairman. It poked fun at the large butts of such repairmen, buttocks that always seem to escape the confines of their pants.

The censor thought bulging buttocks were obscene and ruled it out of the sketch, making the bit irrelevant. Aykroyd bared his behind anyway, and got laughs.

Irreverence, not for everybody

Saturday Night offended some strongly with its irreverence. They received a letter that read: "I've watched your program prior to this and I've found your program to be unsettling and insulting and sadistic. I (my family too) will take no more of your abuse. You've gone too far.... I (my friends and family too) will tell others in our community of your Satanic show. You must all be demons."

After the first few weeks, the show began to grow a following. But only among the youth culture.

The Nielsens were in the basement at an 18 share, but the show attracted large numbers of 18- to 30-year-olds. NBC's sales people used the demographics to attract advertisers, buying *Saturday Night* some time during its first season.

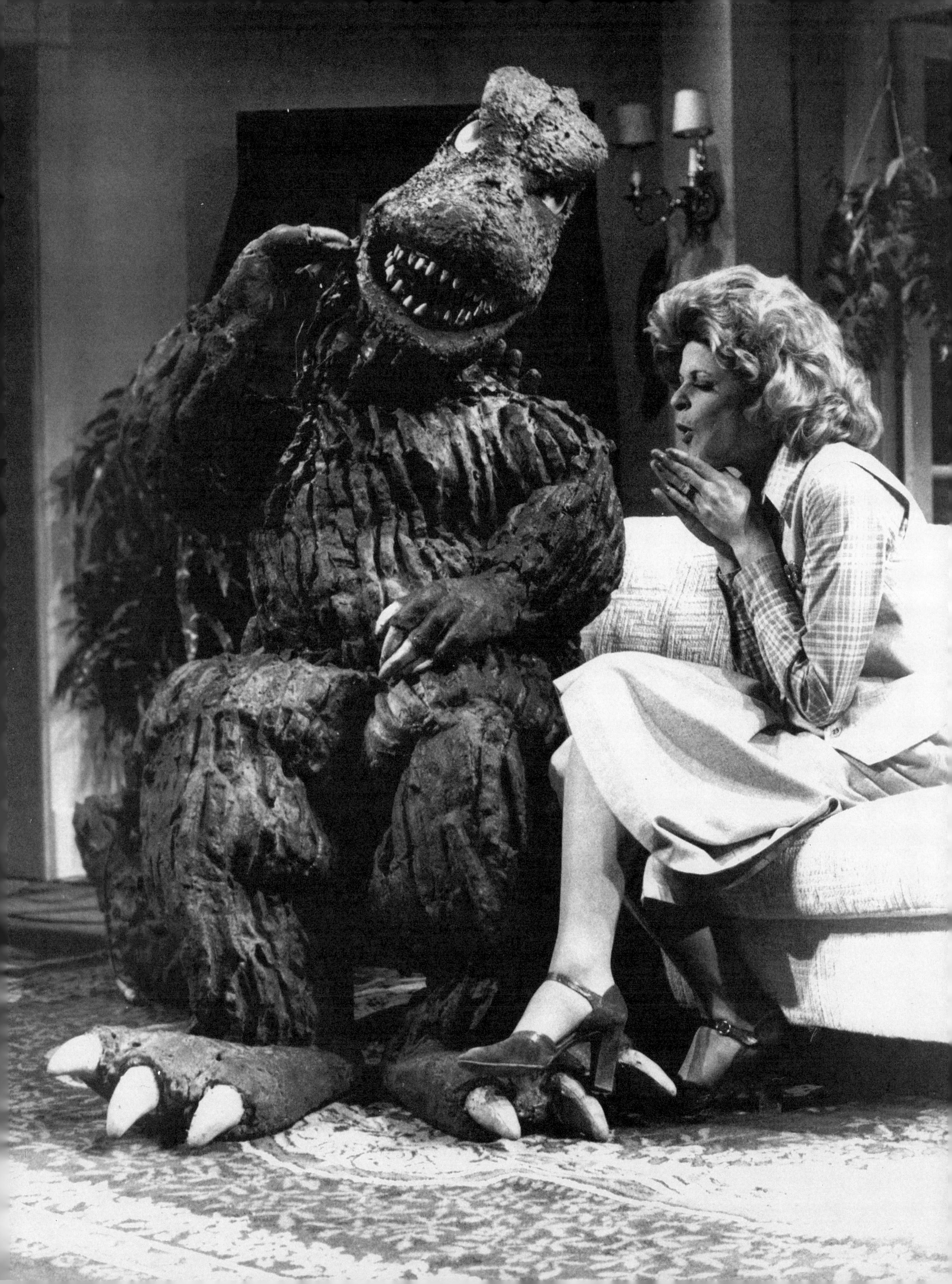

VII

WINNING AWARDS FROM THE ESTABLISHMENT

If demographics bought the show time, the Emmy Award announcements on April 6, 1976 signalled the show was safe. *Saturday Night* picked up five nominations, for best comedy-variety show, best writing, best direction, best graphic design, and—somewhat ironically, but not unexpectedly—best supporting player for Chevy Chase.

Fighting for rep

While *Saturday Night* was struggling out of the cult closet, Chevy Chase over the rest. After the Emmy nominations came out, one network person designed a

> *"The only thing that could fuck it up now is what fucks up everything—success."—Lorne Michaels*

poster for outside 8H. It was a photograph of the cast, but Chase was featured more prominently than the others, and the caption read: "Chevy Chase and The Not-Ready for Prime Time Players."

When he saw it, Lorne Michaels was livid. He ordered it changed.

Fellow player Jane Curtin said, "We were a repertory company, and we knew that repertory companies do not feature one player. We thought we would all shine.

When Chevy became the star, we felt hurt, we felt bad." John Belushi was most disturbed by Chase's popularity. He felt he was getting the short end. "I go where I'm kicked," he said. "They throw me bones dogs wouldn't chew on."

Chase played down his overnight stardom. He told one reporter, "I'm a fad. In this business you can come and go in a second. I could be flushed out tomorrow with a big smile and a handshake."

Chase above the rest

It got worse when Chase made the cover of *New York* magazine. Entertainment insiders came to him to offer advice for his new career. They planted the seed that he could do better away from *Saturday Night*.

His new pal Warren Beatty told him, "You could direct."

The attention seemed to swell his head. He allegedly boasted, "I'll go down to the drugstore, pick up the fan magazines, and I'll bet my name is in more of them than any of yours."

Although Michaels was angered by the poster which featured Chase above the others, he knew where his show was headed. If the viewers wanted Chevy Chase, they got Chevy Chase.

Chase has second thoughts

The falls he took in the "cold opening" increased to the "Fall of the Week". On a show based on spontaneity, regular falls quickly became dull, especially for the writers.

Tom Davis of the *Saturday Night* writing team of Al Franken and Tom Davis, said, "I think we got a little tired of the Fall of the Week a lot sooner than America did."

Weekend Update, another Chevy Chase highlight, was lengthened from 3 to nearly 9 minutes.

As the show's first season was winding up, Chase had serious second thoughts about remaining. Although he was arguably the show's biggest star, he was still only on a writer's contract.

Chase's agent took steps, eventually convincing NBC to pay him an extra $22,000 per season. Chase knew that under Michaels' policy, whatever he got, the other cast got as well. That was unacceptable.

Chase on his own

He got a better deal from NBC. He would go to primetime for three specials at about $500,000 apiece.

The others expected him back for the next season. He didn't say much about the new deal.

Lorne Michaels knew. As the two most prominent creative minds on the show, Chase and Michaels had developed a good friendship. Chase was, in fact, one writer said, a "de facto co-producer."

When Chase bailed, Michaels was thunderstruck. One of those on the show said, "Lorne felt like King Lear: his first daughter had betrayed him." The friendship was over.

Ironically, this contract eruption took place in early May, a week or so before the Emmy ceremony in Hollywood.

Winning respectability at the Emmys

The Emmys brought the show and the network to loggerheads. In the communal spirit of the show, Michaels wanted everyone to fly to Hollywood for the presentation. NBC was horrified at paying so many expenses. Finally, the network relented and paid coach airfare for everyone and $75 a day for expenses.

For the comic radicals Hollywood was the very capital of the Establishment and there was a lot of culture shock. Writer Michael O'Donoghue, who specialized in "death humor", was perhaps the most repugnant of the Establishment. He had insisted the show keep it's hard edge.

When he arrived at the ceremony, his attitude changed. "I remember thinking to myself, 'Why am I fighting this? This is great!' My attitude changed. I embraced television at that moment. Why see *The Carol Burnett Show* take the prize when we were kicking ass?"

Except for the graphic design category, *NBC's Saturday Night* won all of the awards for which it was nominated. It quieted NBC suits still grumbling that the show ought to be cancelled.

There was a lot of attention as Chevy Chase accepted his award that night. "Needless to say, this was totally expected on my part," he quipped. "I'd just like to say that I sort of got a break on that show because of Lorne Michaels. There is a cast of Not Ready for Prime Time Players, all of whom are awful good, and it's been great working with them. And I also would like to thank Ernie Kovacs—I swear—and Lorne Michaels. Thank you."

Very few noticed Chase was speaking about Saturday Night as past history for him. By then, it was.

More conflict at the Emmys

Lorne Michaels found another relationship unraveling during the Emmys. Dick Ebersol had been instrumental in putting *Saturday Night* on the air. Ebersol thought it gave him creative rights over the show, which Michaels didn't agree with at all.

Just before the first show went on, Ebersol suggested Michaels list him in the credits as "executive producer" as a way to say thank you for his help. Not caring too much about formalities, Michaels agreed.

When the NBC top execs saw that credit, they were furious. Suits weren't supposed to take creative credit. The credit was dropped from all future shows.

It became a problem when the Emmys were announced. The Academy takes a show's credits from the first episode of the season. Officially Ebersol was "executive producer" and his name would be the first read if the show won. The day before the awards, some NBC executives cornered Ebersol and had him sign a letter voiding his credit for that first episode. His name wouldn't be called during the presentation.

Still, Michaels thanked Ebersol when he accepted his award. Then again, Chase had thanked Michaels in his acceptance, and now he was gone.

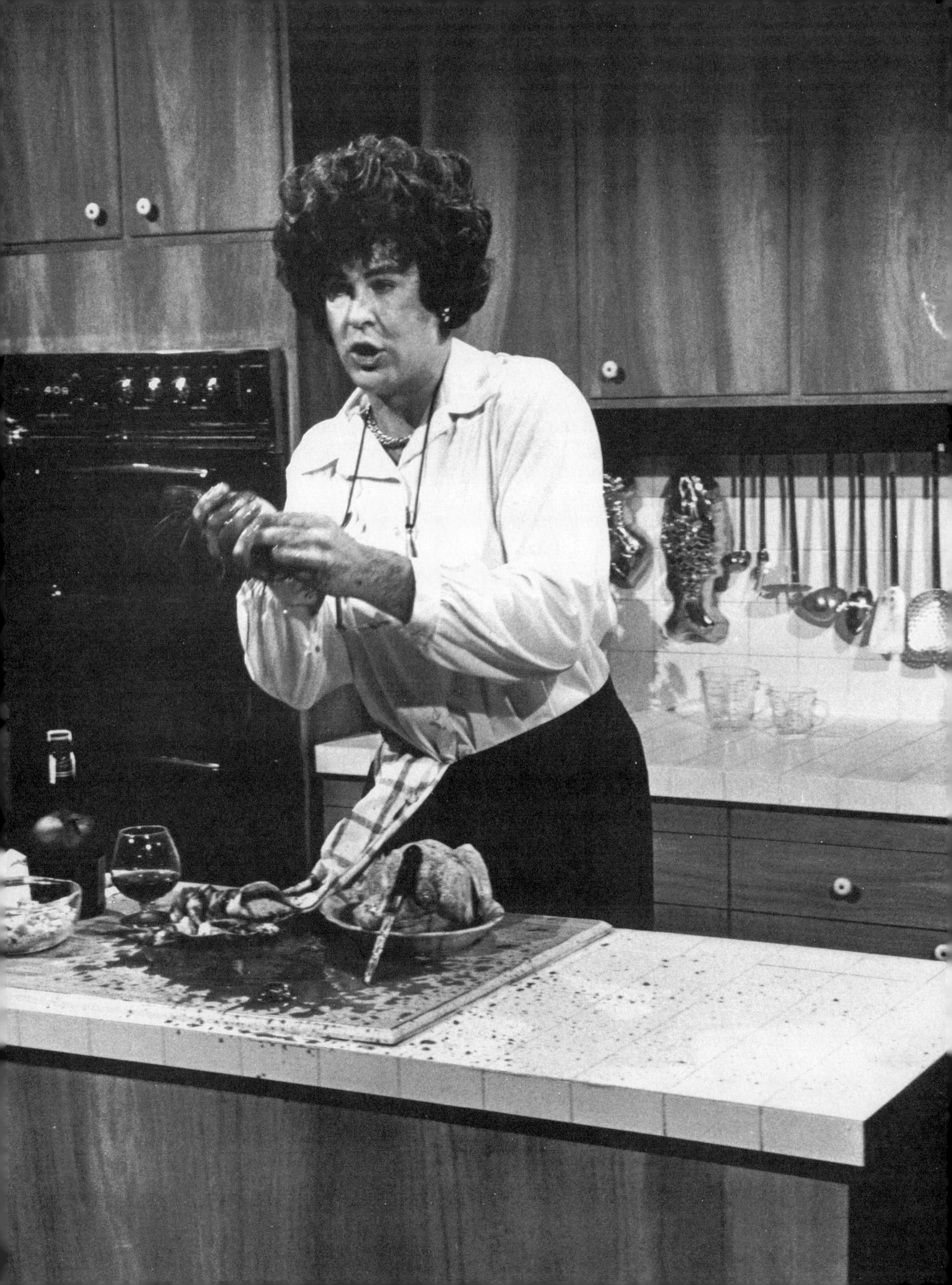

VIII
FIGHTING THE LEGIONS OF DECENCY

Johnny Carson had been

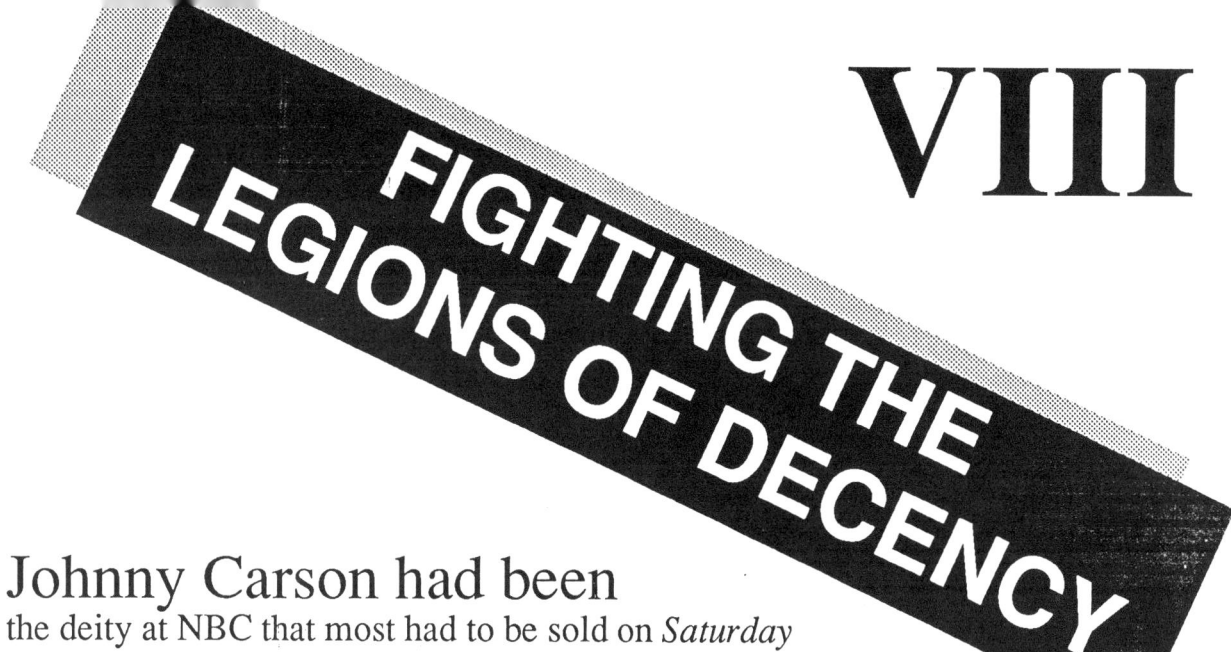

the deity at NBC that most had to be sold on *Saturday Night*;. Late-night was his domain. After meeting Ebersol and Michaels, Carson was cautiously optimistic.

Saturday Night was daring, even a bit licentious by Carson's standards. Raised and trained in burlesque, the risque was not new to Carson. In fact, he rankled his fair share of moralists in his day. Carson reveled in the off-color, but he was suggestive, never blatant.

Leading the way for indecency

Saturday Night was blatant. It was the beginning of new, more open, standards of "decency" on television and in society.

On one *Saturday Night*, Jane Curtin lampooned *The Tonight Show*, the sacred beacon of television entertainment. As co-anchor of Weekend Update, she reported that *The Tonight Show* was returning to a live format, after "doing the show dead for fifteen years."

> *"I've seen some very clever things on the show and they have some very bright young people,"* Carson said. *"But basically they do a lot of drug jokes, a lot of what I would consider sophomoric humor and a lot of stuff I find exceptionally cruel, under the guise of being hip."*

Johnny Carson was the King of Midnight, and the Not Ready for Prime Time Players on *Saturday Night Live* were in his late-night kingdom. The monarch was not amused.

"I've seen some very clever things on the show and they have some very bright young people," Carson said. "But basically they do a lot of drug jokes, a lot of what I would consider sophomoric humor and a lot of stuff I find exceptionally cruel, under the guise of being hip . . . . One night the show ended a minute and a half early. There were 8 people—8 people—standing there onstage and not one of them could think of anything to say. They can't ad-lib a fart at a bean-eating contest."

Putting fuel on the fire

When Chevy Chase took prominence over the other actors, *New York* magazine called the young comedian the next Johnny Carson. The suggestion was Chase replace Carson when the host retired. To a young and successful Chase, that just wasn't hip. "I'd never be tied down for five years interviewing TV personalities," Chase explained.

Johnny Carson biographer Laurence Leamer put it this way, "Johnny was the establishment. The establishment always condemns the young for their bad taste and bad manners; what it fears is their youth, energy, and innovation. The young, for their part, imagine that they will never compromise, never settle into the routines of their elders."

Carson made a point of keeping *Saturday Night*'s regulars off his show. He would hype stars from competing networks night after night, but he wouldn't have on any of the stars from the new series which saved *The Tonight Show* from its Saturday night ignominy. Chase did not only never succeed Carson, he didn't appear as a guest until after he left *Saturday Night*. Gilda Radner didn't appear with Carson until 1983.

"It was trouble between me and Johnny," Chase later admitted. "It was not because we had any anger or rancor between us. Nobody ever came to me to talk about taking over *The Tonight Show*. It was just always in the press. At that time I didn't feel that hosting *The Tonight Show* was the direction I was going in, and I didn't voice it in a nice way. All I had to do was write Johnny a letter, apologizing for any remarks I may have made, and say, 'I think you're great,' and say, 'I want to be on the show.'"

The young turks grow older

By then, all the original young mavericks from *Saturday Night* had gotten older. Many had become movie stars.

Curtin starred in a traditional sitcom. Chase was winning roles as older, establishment yuppies.

He finally subbed for Carson in 1986, and realized firsthand what he had once dismissed was actually extremely difficult. "It was very tough to be the guest host," Chase remembered. "I had just come out of a rehabilitation clinic, and I was a little nervous.

"The monologue was tough, because I had never done one in my life. I had put it together very fast. The most difficult were the interviews. Johnny has a philosophy about his guests. It's basically if you make your guests look good, you look good. I tell you, it's tough. He listens very carefully and he responds well, and he has obviously caught the heart of Middle America. It's tough."

Paul Corkery, another Carson biographer, says that now Carson and Chase play poker together. Corkery said, "Johnny really doesn't hold a grudge."

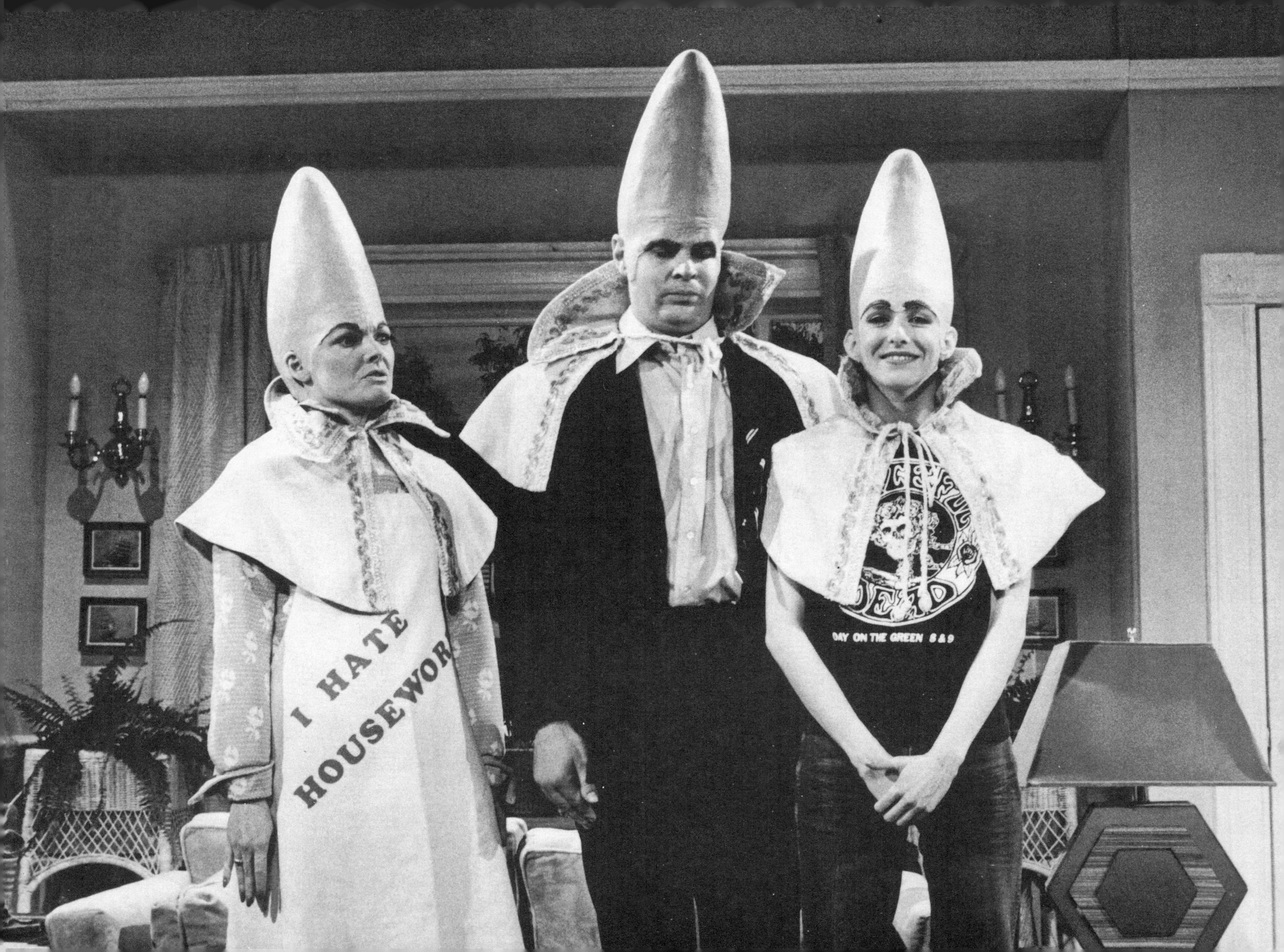
I HATE
HOUSEWOR
DAY ON THE GREEN 8 & 9

IX

NOW IT WOULD BE SATURDAY NIGHT LIVE

The Emmys had been a triumph for the show. Cancellation was no longer a fear.

When the second season began, NBC doubled the *Saturday Night* budget. The show still went over budget by about $25,000 a week, but Michaels didn't have to fight the network as hard to approve the overages. They usually went through without a question.

A new name for the second season

Now it was called *Saturday Night Live*. Howard Cosell's effort at ABC died during its first season. The cancellation freed the name "Saturday Night Live", which had been Michaels' original choice. He took it.

Even with a new name and a bigger budget, there was fear Chevy Chase's departure would hurt the show. NBC negotiated with Chase to keep him for the first few shows of the second season to provide continuity.

> *The censor also didn't like their use of "ass" to describe a donkey in a Nativity scene. Writer Anne Beatts said, "We've used that word before," to which the censor responded, "Not in front of Mary and Joseph."*

Chase appeared in smaller and smaller doses until disappearing altogether. In one of his last "falls of the week", Chase finally injured himself, hurting—of all things—his testicles.

Filling the void

Michaels needed to fill the void after Chase left. Cosell's cancellation made Bill Murray available.

Murray had originally auditioned for *SNL* but lost out to Belushi. Michaels now had his opportunity to hire Murray, but wanted to avoid direct comparisons between Chase and Murray. He didn't want Murray to be considered a second-banana usurping Chase's talent.

Bill Murray first appeared on the show on January 15, 1977, five shows after Chase left. He certainly didn't appear to be a Chevy Chase replacement.

Chase was known for his preppy looks and innocent delivery. Murray was described as "the kid in the gang comedies who rode the motorcycle . . . the guy you hated looking at."

Murray was a ball of hyper angry energy. One of his dinner activities was pressing sandwiches through his fingers. He walked around the offices and the studio with a bottle of whiskey in one hand. Often he engaged in tickle fights with the women on the show.

"There's some danger involved . . . something in Bill's eyes," Michaels admitted.

Murray carves out his turf

Murray gave his performances his all, making his own personality palpable. He still got angry letters from Chevy Chase fans.

After Chase left, Weekend Update was without an anchor. Jane Curtin filled the role, and she experienced the closest comparison to Chase. She received many negative letters, mostly based on sex appeal.

To address this problem, during Update she said she thought journalism should be based on professionalism and not sex. She then ripped open her blouse and said, "Try these on for size, Connie Chung!"

One positive effect of Chase's departure was the establishment of the repertory. Popularity seemed more evenly distributed.

Among the cast, Murray was accepted, and it showed. He and Aykroyd made believable right-wing ex-cops in a sketch where the two come across an apartment shared by two women. The ex-cops believe they are lesbians, enter the home, and beat them to death. They end by announcing, "Another homosexuality-related death." The show received plenty of mail from gay groups for that one.

Murray's one of the Nerds

One of Murray's more memorable—and more likable—roles was the recurring character of Todd, half of the Nerds. Gilda Radner played the other half, Nerd Lisa Loopner. The Nerds were two nice high school kids who just didn't fit in, but who had a charming friendship. Jane Curtin often played Mrs. Loopner, Lisa's mother. At the end of each Nerds bit, Todd rubs Lisa's head in a move called "noogies," to show affection. It was part of the charm.

A Nerds sketch got the show into its biggest fight with the censors. In "Nerds Nativity", for the December 22, 1979 show, Todd and Lisa take part in the high school Christmas pageant. The censors didn't like Todd's characterization of Lisa as the only girl in school "physically correct" to play the Virgin Mary. The censor also didn't like their use of "ass" to describe a donkey. Writer Anne Beatts said, "We've used that word before," to which the censor responded, "Not in front of Mary and Joseph."

The censor went on to say, "You cannot spoof the nativity." The network didn't understand that it wasn't the nativity they were satirizing but second-rate pageants in which the angels have paper plate halos.

The censors also objected to the "noogies" that evening. "You can't give noogies to the Virgin Mary," complained the censor.

"But she's not the Virgin Mary!" said Beatts. "She's Gilda Radner playing Lisa Loopner playing the Virgin Mary with a paper plate on her head!"

The sketch was rewritten at the last minute. Radner and Murray had to read all their lines from cue cards. Still, the noogies stayed.

Internal politics of the cast

Murray meshed with the rising dominant personalities in the cast, Aykroyd and Belushi. All three appreciated the out-of-control tough guy mentality.

"They were," said one writer, "bad-assed, macho, go-get-'em bravado types. They were formidable in that way, and their charisma came out of that as well. They weren't the crying, sensitive males—this was not that brand."

Another writer said of Belushi, "He was mad at everybody, or something was wrong. He would talk about anything, like an actor talking. Like a tornado that would spin itself round and round and then be exhausted."

Increasing drug use sent Belushi out of control. On more than one occasion, a staff member had to look for Belushi when he skipped out just before show time.

Aykroyd bonded with Belushi in an almost brotherly way. They shared an office known as "the Cave", for the mess of food, dirty laundry and other forgotten refuse lying about. He pleaded with Belushi to put himself together. To no avail.

Violence on Saturday night, live

Drugs weren't the only catalyst to violence. Chevy Chase came back in the third season for the first time as host. It was during a ratings "sweep" period and his appearance gave the show a good boost.

By this time, Curtin had been hosting Update successfully for more than a year. When Chase came back, he wanted to do it solo. The two had heated words. Lorne Michaels intervened, making them co-anchors.

This strained feelings. Bill Murray was already smarting over the initial assault he took from fans comparing him unfavorably with Chase. This led to a shouting match between Chase and Murray which escalated into a fist fight only minutes before air time.

"This is my show now!" Murray yelled. The men were separated and the show went on, and garnered *SNL*'s highest ratings at the time.

Even Dan Aykroyd, whose characters were the epitome of comic serenity and intellect, has been know to fly into a rage. In the third season, NBC executive Rick Traum sent the *SNL* staff a memo requesting reimbursement to the network for $400 in unauthorized expenses. Aykroyd spray-painted graphitti in an elevator, saying "I will kill you, Rick."

The show was rising in the ratings and had just won its second batch of Emmys. NBC didn't want to jeopardize its winning show, so no word of Aykroyd's deed was made. It was quietly cleaned up.

All of this energy was put to constructive purposes, too. Several new skits and characters evolved.

Coneheads from France

Dan Aykroyd turned his obsession with UFOs into The Coneheads. The Coneheads were a family of aliens from Remulak living on Earth. The actors played the characters with latex cones on their heads.

Aykroyd played Conehead father Beldar, Jane Curtin played his wife, Prymaat, and Laraine Newman took the part of their daughter Connie. The Coneheads—who told others they were from "France"—tried to adapt to Middle American life.

Beldar often told his guests to "consume mass quantities" of food. In one bit, guest host Frank Zappa plays a rocker taking Connie out for a date. Curtin as Conehead mother Prymaat tells her daughter to return at "the correct time coordinates."

The Coneheads mocked straightlaced sitcom families. They hit big with audiences.

More ongoing skits and characters

Belushi was making a name for himself with his Samurai character as well as the owner of the Greek diner: "Cheeseburger, cheeseburger . . . no Coke, Pepsi!"

The Weekend Update became more popular, with Bill Murray playing a suave vapid entertainment reporter. Aykroyd played opposite Curtin in "Point/Counterpoint" mock-debate segments. Aykroyd finished arguments with: "Jane, you ignorant slut!"

It was for Update that Radner created Roseanne Rosannadanna, a commentator who grossed out anchor Curtin with digressing lectures on hair in a boil of soup or rat droppings in a sandwich. She ended each commentary with: "It's always *somethin'*!" and the line became famous.

Outside of Update, Dan Aykroyd created the Czech brothers with Steve Martin. The brothers, Jorge and Yortuck Festrunk came to America to seek "swinging" free sex. Aykroyd and Martin's cheesy accents and leering at "foxes" played by Radner, Curtin, and Newman was an instant hit parodying the '70s sexuality.

It would be with another certain pair of "brothers" that Dan Aykroyd would gain his immortality with John Belushi, the Blues Brothers, Jake and Elwood.

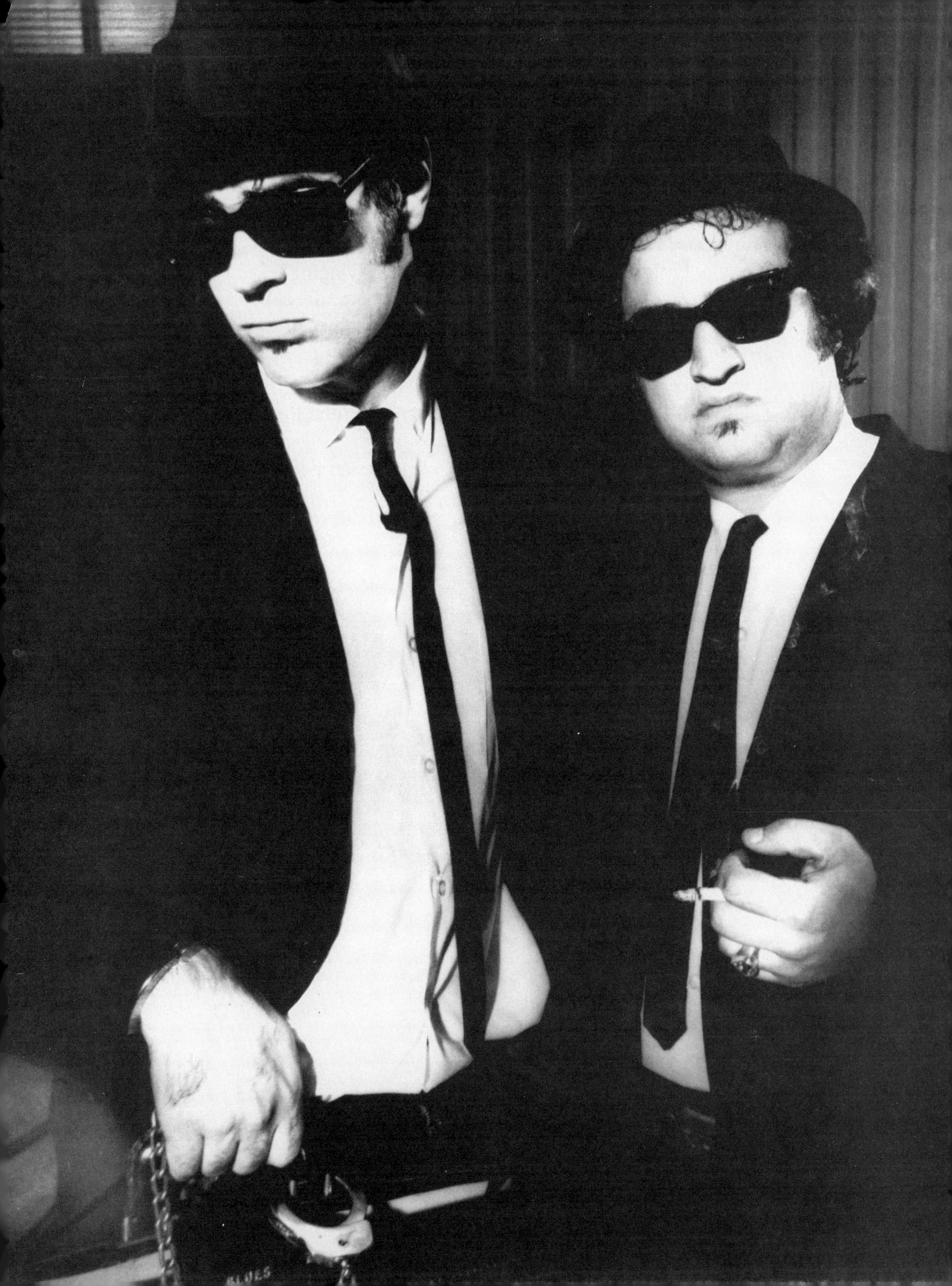

THE BLUES BROTHERS

It began as a poke at the Bee costumes.

When, in the first season, Dan Aykroyd and John Belushi performed an old blues number, "King Bee," Elwood and Joliet Jake were born. They weren't just another set of characters; they were individuals. It wasn't Aykroyd and Belushi as Elwood and Jake, but just Elwood and Jake.

"I mean, *who* are they?" asked a *Rolling Stone* reporter. "Jake, for example, looks a fuck of a lot like John Bel— -"

"Now *listen*," intoned Atlantic Records executive Michael Klenfner, "I don't know any more about them than you do. All I know is they sound great and act awfully goddamned strange."

> *"I mean, who are they?" asked a Rolling Stone reporter. "Jake, for example, looks a fuck of a lot like John Bel---"*
>
> *"Now listen," intoned Atlantic Records executive Michael Klenfner, "I don't know any more about them than you do. All I know is they sound great and act awfully goddamned strange."*

<u>Beyond Saturday night</u>

Although they appeared on *Saturday Night Live*, and delivered a blistering rendition of "Soul Man", the Blues Brothers were not truly a part of the show. They were independent.

Jake and Elwood opened for Steve Martin at the Los Angeles Amphitheater. A record was born.

They brought in a cooking band and recorded an album, *Briefcase Full of Blues*. The band consisted of *SNL* band leader Paul Shaffer on keyboards, Steve Cropper and Matt Murphy on guitar, Donald "Duck" Dunn on bass, a horn section of saxophones, trumpets, and trombone. The late Bill Graham, concert promoter extraordinaire, proclaimed, "What a goddamned good band!"

The album sold more than a million copies. A Blues Brothers movie was on the horizon.

Elwood—or was it Dan Aykroyd—wrote the script. "The Scriptatron XL 9000 has to finish the script," Elwood corrected before the Universal film got underway.

The making of the movie

Jake was a little more forthcoming. "We play ourselves," he explained. "Here's a simple synopsis: it starts with me getting out of jail after three years and I expect the band to still be together...."

"He got three years on a five-year rap," Elwood added. "Armed robbery at a gas station. I was driving but he took the rap because he knew I would string myself up if I went to jail. He did it for the *band*."

"Well, the band demanded their per diem," Jake elaborated, "so I had to rob the place! But anyhow, the film is about finding the band members and trying to get it all back again."

"We hunt them down like cops, like *detectives*," Elwood said. "We have nothing, a scrap of paper with their last phone numbers and a couple of old addresses. We discover that each one now has a different trip; a couple of 'em are living suburban lives, mostly working day jobs. We were just getting hot when Jake went in the slammer, drawing big crowds at highway drinking halls. Now we've reformed to try again."

The Blues Brothers film was one of the biggest of 1980, including appearances by legendary R&B performers including Cab Calloway and Aretha Franklin. That night, when that same *Rolling Stone* reporter again pressed Jake and Elwood on their association with *Saturday Night*, they jumped up and left, commenting, "Well, gotta split now. Er, hope you like the show tonight."

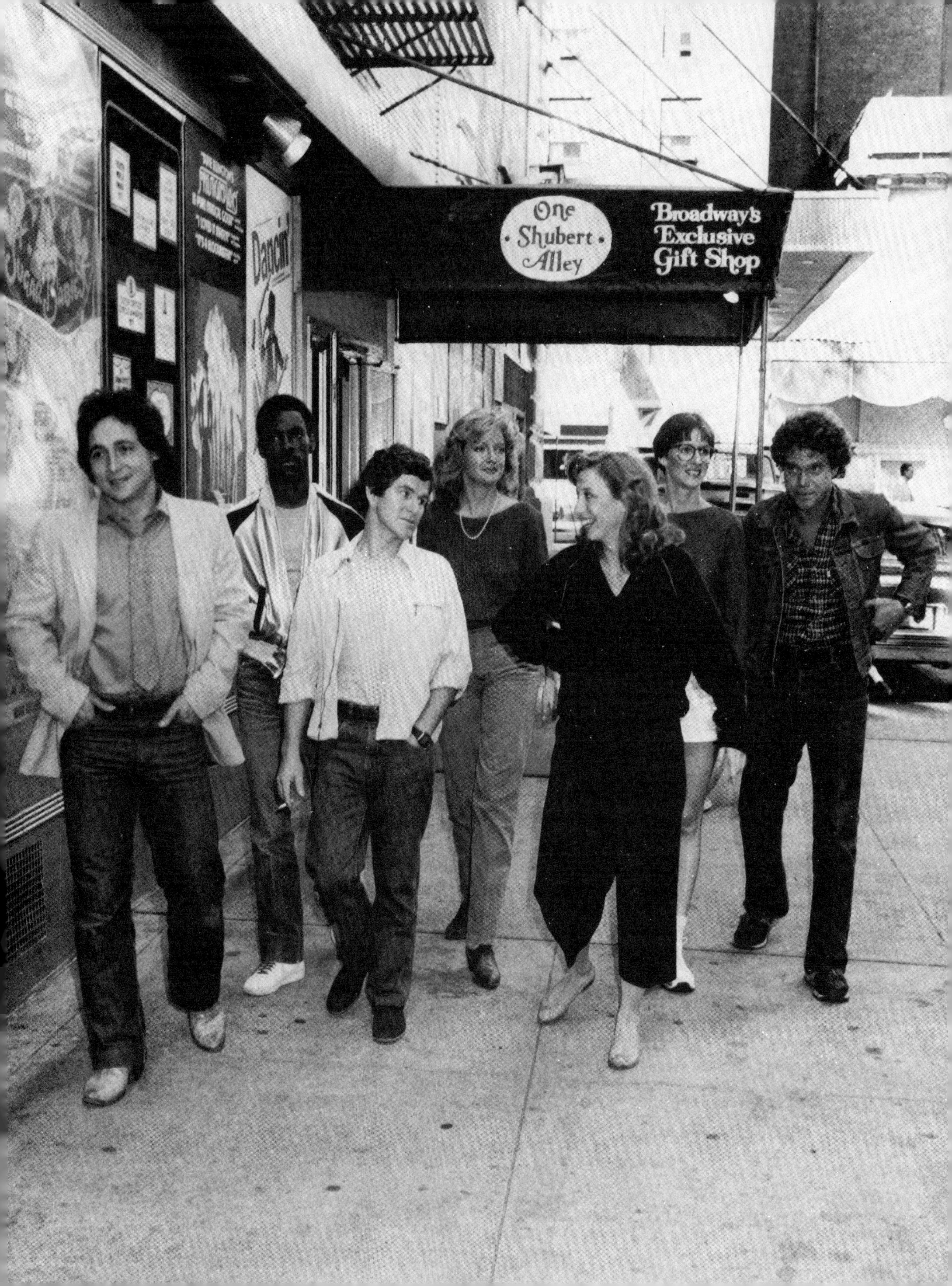

One Shubert Alley
Broadway's Exclusive Gift Shop
Dancin'

XI
FROM UNDERGROUND TO BEAUTIFUL PEOPLE

Saturday Night Live finally lifted itself out of "cult" status. It was now an acknowledged powerhouse.

Lorne Michaels believed *SNL* was essentially less television and more rock'n'roll. Critics even called the show "the Beatles of comedy." Some of the show's "greatest hits" came from the third and fourth seasons.

Perverse Uncle Roy and the girls

Frequent host Buck Henry's recurring character, Uncle Roy, was a child-molesting babysitter. Radner and Newman played the little girls he babysat.

The sketches revolved around perverse "games". For example, the girls hunted for "Buried Treasure" in Roy's pants pockets. They also played "Ruffy the Dog"; the girls spanked Roy for being bad.

> All the "radical underground" comedians came to look more like "beautiful people." One writer on the show said, "Lorne got the apartment, the limo, the driver, the place in Amagansett. The effect it had on all of us was: 'Wait a minute. He's doing all that; why shouldn't we be able to do all of that, too?'"

Popularity brought increasing autonomy from the network. The censors couldn't cut much once *SNL* became a hit. Tempted, they couldn't touch Uncle Roy, and Roy kept getting more perverse.

More innocent skits

Not all the skits were edged. Staff writer Don Novello occasionally appeared as Father Guido Sarducci. The good Father was rock critic for the Vatican newspaper and appeared on Weekend Update.

Sarducci, a low-key character, became one of the show's earliest megahits. The censors worried he would somehow offend Catholics. For instance, for one Update appearance, Sarducci was going to report he had discovered the check from the Last Supper. The censors changed it to the "Last Brunch".

Novello also invented the Greek restaurant sketches based on a real restaurant in Chicago, the Billy Goat. It was routine, with little change, but Belushi made it a hit.

Then there was the inimitable "Mr. Bill". Mr. Bill satirized children's cartoons. He was a clay doll in films made by Walter Williams.

Williams had sent the show an unsolicited tape. Michaels played it to great response, then hired Williams to produce Mr. Bill regularly.

Mr. Bill films didn't change much each time. He was always clobbered and destroyed by Mr. Sluggo and Mr. Hands. The first film cost $20 to make, but after Michaels hired him, he used his budget of $1,500 a sketch.

Rising in the ratings war

In its first year, *SNL* struggled to get better than a 20 ratings share while other shows averaged a 30. Chevy Chase's third season return as host brought the highest ratings at the time, a 38 share.

In the fourth season, the show *averaged* a 39 share every week. NBC estimated the audience rose from 7.5 million people a week during the first season to 25 million during the fourth.

John Belushi had become a "star" in the *SNL* cast, much as Chase was three years before. His presence attracted viewers.

Belushi appeared in the outrageous and successful film, *Animal House*. He brought his film character, Bluto, to *Saturday Night Live*. The fans followed, joining what Lorne Michaels called the "undeserved audience."

A moneymaker for NBC

Saturday Night Live became one of NBC's few money-making shows in its forth season. It was the sweetest revenge on all the suits who had questioned Lorne Michaels' vision.

NBC's ad sales department had a hard time selling commercial spots for $7,500 during *SNL*'s first year. Ad sales increased when the demographic report revealed the audience of target young people. In its fourth season, thirty-second spots on *SNL* sold for $50,000 to $60,000 apiece. Affiliate stations carrying the show increased from only 144 to almost all at 215.

Lorne Michaels and the SNL cast benefitted. Michaels take shot up to $1.5 million in salary alone, along with bonuses and "development funds" from NBC. He set up his own company, Broadway Video. Michaels also began producing *Best of Saturday Night* specials for NBC.

His senior writers earned salaries of $200,000 to $300,000. The cast, offered almost nothing during the first year, now each pulled in half a million dollars.

The show's budget was raised to $553,000 per show for the fifth season. For the first time, the show came in under budget.

Changes, and more changes of success

Blues Brothers had been Ackroyd's and Belushi's creation independent of Michaels and *SNL*. Everyone started to hold out for a genuine *Saturday Night* movie.

The show became such a phenomenon, the title "Not Ready for Prime Time Players" was dropped in the fourth season. The cast were simply deemed, "the stars."

Writers and stars renegotiated their contracts—and occasionally made unusual demands. The writing team of Franken and Davis insisted that the restrooms by their office constantly be supplied with fresh towels. If towels weren't available, NBC would be fined and those fines would buy more towels. Another writer insisted a hospital bed be installed in her office.

More than money or perks, the cast and crew became genuine superstars. Other superstars wanted to be members of the studio audience. Luminaries such as David Bowie, John Lithgow, Richard Dreyfus, Mikhail Barisnikov, and Jack Nicholson called for tickets.

Paul McCartney offered Belushi $6,000 to perform his hilarious Joe Cocker impersonation at his birthday party. Belushi happily took him up on the offer.

From Underground to Beautiful People

Michaels bought a luxury house in Amagansett. He held polo parties for rich and famous friends.

All the "radical underground" comedians came to look more like "beautiful people." One writer on the show said, "Lorne got the apartment, the limo, the driver, the place in Amagansett. The effect it had on all of us was:

'Wait a minute. He's doing all that; why shouldn't we be able to do all of that, too?'"

Of course, the stars lost all their privacy. When several cast members went to Minnesota for a "peaceful" vacation together, they found their cabin surrounded by fans. The stars had to jump out a back window to escape.

Jane Curtin disliked the hype and permanently donned dark glasses and big hats. Belushi was enamored with fame, but his friend Aykroyd wasn't fond of it. Aykroyd would walked streets several feet behind Belushi to let Belushi get mobbed.

Not all stars are equal

Not all of the stars reaped the glory. Laraine Newman and Garrett Morris fell behind. They had been overshadowed.

Morris was given stereotypical "black" roles. He played black women in drag: Tina Turner, Diana Ross, and Pearl Bailey. One co-worker said the others on the show made Morris "participate in his own degradation."

Things came to a head when Cicely Tyson hosted the show. Before Tyson came out for the opening monologue, Morris appeared dressed as Tyson. When the real Tyson came out, she asked what he was doing. He explained that he thought the Tyson part was for him.

"I was hired by this show," Morris said, "under the terms the Token Minority Window Dressing Act of 1968." He played "all parts darker than Tony Orlando."

In the same vein of Belushi's Bee tirade against Rob Reiner, Cicely Tyson said, "Garrett, what is happening to you? Look at what you're doing! When we worked together at the Black Resentment Drama Workshop in the 1960s, I expected something really very big from you . . . . Where's your integrity? You have talent and you're just throwing it away . . . . What are you doing it for? Money?"

Morris responded, "Well, it doesn't look bad on my resume, and I get to keep the dresses."

His one stereotypical role fans remembered was when he played baseball player Chico Escuela. His appearances on Weekend Update consisted of: "Base-boll has been berry, berry good to me."

The show gathers no moss

Success became tangible when the Rolling Stones appeared as guest host. Michaels made sure everything would be perfect.

The cast upstaged the Stones. In one sketch, Dan Aykroyd played talk show host Tom Snyder interviewing Mick Jagger as Mick Jagger.

As Snyder, Aykroyd said he could move with the best of them. When he began hopping around like Jagger, Aykroyd was clearly upstaging the singer. Jagger made a few lame comments about the wig Aykroyd used as Snyder.

SNL had clearly become more rock'n'roll than television.

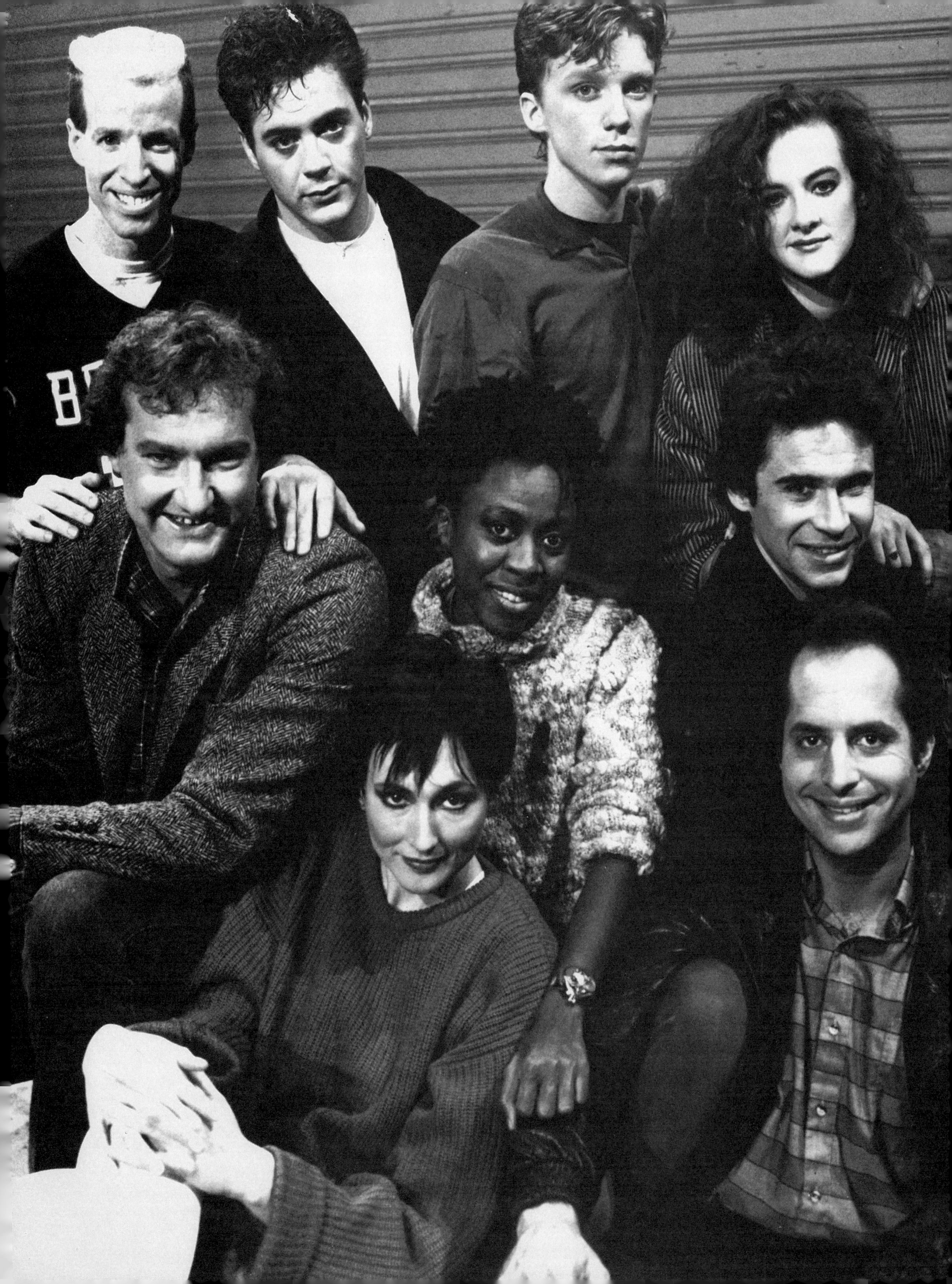

XII

THE LOVE CHILDREN ALL FOUND AGENTS

Saturday Night Live had climbed to the top.

The only direction left was down.

Michaels had once said that only success could ruin the show.

Now they would find out.

Success ruins the radicals

The comedy radicals had gone Hollywood. "We were afraid of them," said one production assistant of the cast and writers. "To knock on a door and ask for a script you could get your head bitten off." Another concurred, saying, "There was a certain pride taken in not treating people well."

> "The Love Children had agents. In the beginning it was like hippies working on a commune. Then people became much more conscious of their own worth and success, of what they were getting paid or not getting paid, and everybody began to pursue money. The hippies turned into financial wizards."

The press attacked the show, not without reason. While *TV Guide* reporter John Mariani prepared a story on the show, he approached Bill Murray for an interview. Murray asked if the story would be focused on him or the entire cast. Mariani said it would be about everybody, and Murray turned him down. Mariani said, "They become paranoid about people wanting something from them."

The truth about drugs

Drugs were a given. The actors took drugs; the writers and producers took drugs. Much to the disdain of NBC, much of the humor on the show revolved around the hipness of drugs.

It started with marijuana. As the show became more successful, cocaine took its place. Many on the show were heavy users, more than a gram a day in some cases.

Not all partook: Curtin didn't, Radner didn't. Radner called it the "devil's dandruff." She had been stricken with an eating disorder, bulimia. She once joked with a reporter that she had thrown up in all of the bathrooms in Rockefeller Center.

Coke was the major catalyst of personality changes. One woman connected to the show said, "Coke takes the heart right out of people. It's irrelevant if you're hurting somebody."

Losing their proletarian roots

One of the writers said, "*Saturday Night* became a breeding ground for stars, and people were looking for where they could cash in." Another writer commented on the irony of the attitude change by saying, "The Love Children had agents. In the beginning it was like hippies working on a commune. Then people became much more conscious of their own worth and success, of what they were getting paid or not getting paid, and everybody began to pursue money. The hippies turned into financial wizards."

As the show grew popular, corporations wanted to cash in. One company wanted to create a *Saturday Night* breakfast cereal, another a toothpaste. McDonalds wanted to market Rosanne Rosannadanna drinking glasses.

Mr. Bill goes to court

Even Walter Williams, creator of Mr. Bill, wasn't immune. He saw people manufacturing illegal Mr. Bill buttons, posters, and other junk. He ignored it until he heard from a Mr. Vance de Generes. De Generes had been the "Mr. Hands" in the original Mr. Bill sketch. He demanded a large sum of money from Williams as a settlement.

Williams took it to court and won; de Generes was awarded only a small amount. The hearing could've been an *SNL* sketch. The judge wore a "Mr. Sluggo" name pin on his robe. He placed a clay model of Mr. Bill, and took out a pair of scissors, cutting the Mr. Bill model in half, throwing the head to de Generes and the body to Williams. The spectators got into the act by chanting, "Oh, no, Mr. Bill."

Belushi wants to go independent

The show had bigger problems. They weren't solved with humor.

Belushi decided he had outgrown the show, much as Chevy Chase had a few years earlier. He tasted fame and fortune with *Animal House* and the Blues Brothers and was eager to work independently.

His doubts grew when he made the film *1941* with Dan Aykroyd. More and more, he had to split his time between Hollywood and New York, and Hollywood was winning.

Belushi took on a superior air, fueled by drugs. One person on the show said he was "surprised when someone spoke in his presence without his permission, that sort of thing."

Another said, "John in the fourth year was doing a lot of drugs, and was very exhausted, pushed to the physical limit, crisscrossing the country. He was scary around the office. You never knew when he'd turn."

At one point, he attacked Al Franken and had to be held back. During one show, he was in Hollywood. He sent back a little film with him in the pool of his friend, director John Landis. Surrounded by girls, Belushi said, "I'd really love to be there."

Michaels didn't use the film. That helped Belushi decide. He wouldn't be back for a fifth season.

Dan Aykroyd decides to call it quits

The real question was whether Dan Aykroyd would be back. He was torn between the show and his friendship with Belushi. In the end a comment made by writer Michael O'Donoghue about Belushi's drug use offended Aykroyd and decided he wouldn't come back.

Some say it was just the lure of the Big Time, films such as *1941*, and, of course, the *Blues Brothers*, which he was writing at the time. One writer observed, "The feeling was definitely that John spirited Danny away from the show."

There didn't appear to be as much animosity between *SNL* and Aykroyd as there had been with Chevy Chase. In his departure press release, Aykroyd said, "Lorne is a visionary whose guidance and friendship account for a great deal of my success. He supports his staff and lets each writer carry his or her scene through to air time."

Michaels, for his part, said, "Danny is a highly honorable man, and I think it pained him to leave."

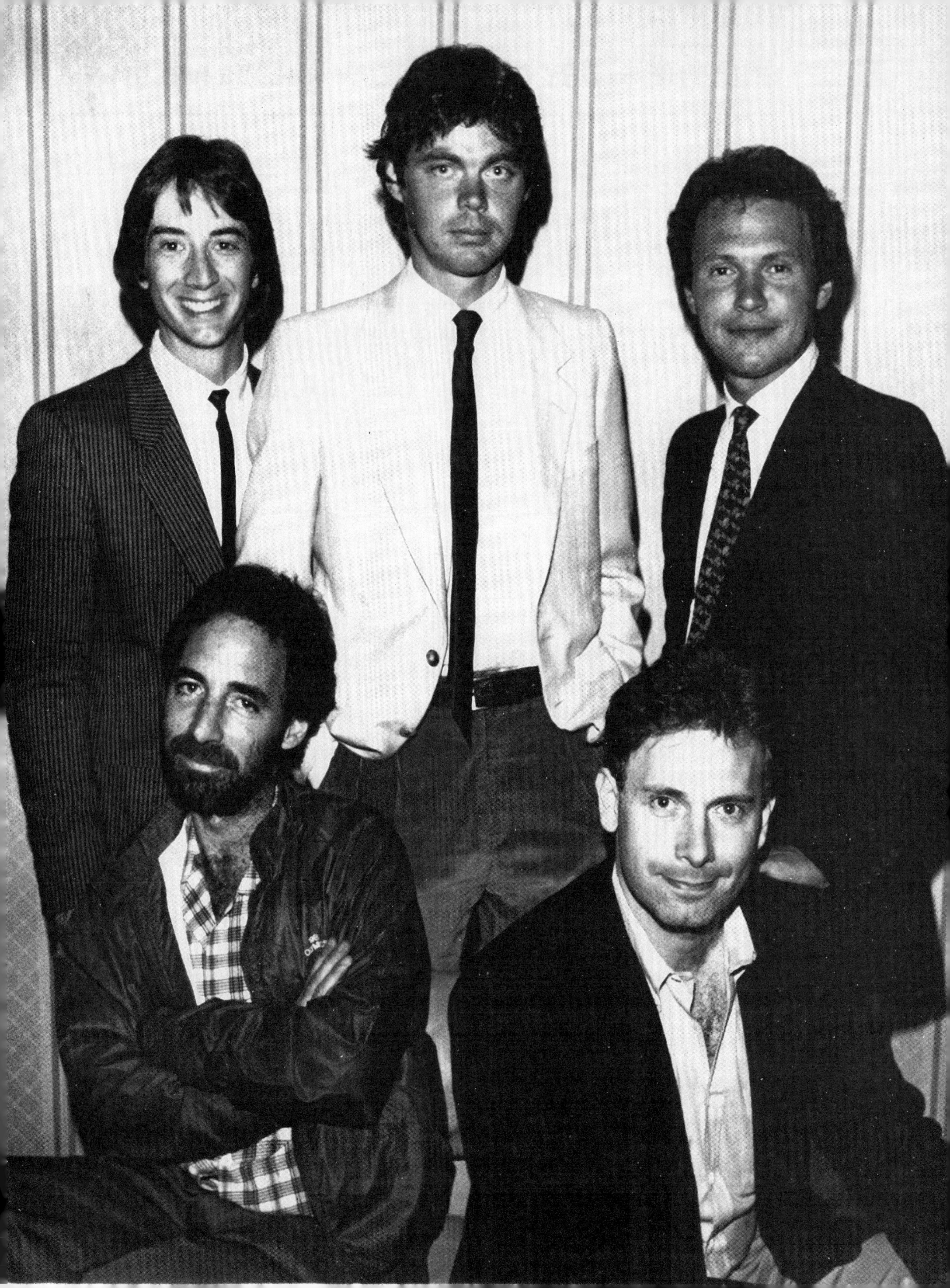

XIII

LORNE MICHAELS ENDS HIS REIGN

The fifth season began with *SNL* in disarray.

When the Blues Brothers album sold more than a million copies, Lorne Michaels wanted to fight back. He and Paul Shaffer produced an album of Gilda Radner, *Gilda Radner, Live From New York*.

Dueling egos

One employee of the show called the battle of the albums "dueling egos." The quality was inferior, but they wouldn't give up.

The material was reworked into a Broadway show and, later, a film. The Broadway show sold some tickets, but critics were savage.

> Harry Shearer called the show "a highly complex, highly political hierarchic structure masquerading as a college dorm. I couldn't share the myth. I wasn't that dumb."

It was Radner's *Saturday Night Live* routine and critics wondered why the public should pay top dollar on Broadway when they could see the same thing on television for free.

Between that defeat and the departures of Aykroyd and Belushi, there was great pessimism during the fifth season. Success *had* ruined the show.

Fifth season host Teri Garr said, "All you heard was bitching and moaning. Everyone was complaining." The writers kept observing how great it would be to have had Aykroyd or Belushi play parts.

Murray becomes a temperamental star

Bill Murray became the leading male after Aykroyd and Belushi left. Those who worked with him say he became the sort of temperamental star Belushi and Chevy Chase had been. One observed, he was "pissed off the whole time, pissed at the writers, pissed at the producer, pissed at the network, pissed at TV in general."

Murray got his first taste of independent fame with his first film, *Meatballs*. It fared respectably at the box office.

With Radner subdued by her Broadway failure, Murray and Jane Curtin became the standouts. Michaels hired Harry Shearer, a member of the comedy improvisation group, The Credibility Gap. He also had written for series such as *Laverne and Shirley*.

Politics masquerading as a college dorm

From the moment he came aboard, Shearer joined those Garr called "bitching and moaning." Shearer didn't like the office politics established years before he arrived. He called them, "a highly complex, highly political hierarchic structure masquerading as a college dorm. I couldn't share the myth. I wasn't that dumb."

That strain made work more difficult. Nobody put as much into the show anymore. Most knew the show was on its last legs; the fifth season would be the last. Writer Alan Zweibel remarked, "Everyone was looking beyond the show. 'Gee, maybe the party is going to end. Is there going to be another party that I'll be invited to? What next?'"

One writer called *Saturday Night Live* during that year "a wobbling kind of machine." The show had always been uneven in quality; now it was more pronounced.

Curtin turned in wonderful characters, but the sketches were grade-school humor. One took place in a "vomitorium," and starred the host of the week, Burt Reynolds.

Despair and personal problems

Garrett Morris and Laraine Newman hadn't found the fame of their co-workers. They were completely lost in season five. This turned to despair and personal problems.

Newman developed anorexia and used drugs. Morris' drug use ruined him.

He became delusional, insisting he saw an "invisible hypnotist robot." In this state, it was dangerous to put him on live. He frequently was written out of sketches. That only made him worse.

The roles he got weren't any better than the stereotypes and drag queens of the past. Except for Chico Escuela, he played butlers and monkey-men.

Silverman spells doom for SNL

SNL was doomed when Fred Silverman replaced Herb Schlosser as NBC president. Silverman hated having a successful show he didn't understand. It was making too much money to cancel, though.

One exec who worked with him said, "Fred did not understand the dynamic of *Saturday Night*—the attitude of the people who made it and the attitude of its viewers. He totally didn't understand why *Saturday Night* was a hit: It was so anti everything else on TV, it didn't conform to the rules."

Silverman's critics say he believed in "lowest common denominator" programming. At ABC his strategy had consisted of spin-offs from successful shows and "jiggle programming", using good-looking, well-endowed women. He used this approach for Charlie's *Angels*.

Wednesday night at nine is Gilda Time!

Ratings at NBC were slipping badly. Almost the only successful show was *SNL*.

Silverman wanted to milk the property by making the show conform to his rules. He wanted to spin off Gilda Radner into his next prime time hit by creating her own variety vehicle on Wednesday nights. Silverman was ecstatic at the prospect, constantly repeating: "Wednesday night at nine is Gilda Time!"

Silverman approached Michaels and Radner, but they weren't interested. They were too tired after five years of *SNL* and the disaster of Radner on Broadway.

Silverman was astounded. He couldn't believe they were turning down the wonderful opportunity. After that, he was no friend of *Saturday Night Live*.

Making fun of the network president

He didn't understand the show didn't need or want him as a friend. They were successful. In fact they satirized Silverman.

One of the worst was by Al Franken, who had begun appearing as a commentator on Weekend Update. In "Limo for the Lamo" Franken asks for limousine service because he was one of NBC's "few bright spots". He complains that Fred Silverman got a limo even though he was "a total, unequivocal failure".

When Michaels saw Franken's monologue against Silverman, he didn't think it was very funny, but let it go. Before Franken read the sketch on the air, Silverman's assistant read it, and said: "It's really going to hurt him."

Silverman, already in trouble with the network over losing ratings, was incensed. That same assistant reported that after seeing "Limo for a Lamo," Silverman asked, "How could he do that to me?"

Michaels tries to save his show

Despite the show's tumbling to a halt, Lorne Michaels wanted it to continue. The entire cast was leaving after the fifth season. Michaels saw it as an opportunity, but obstacles stood in his path.

The Silverman satires had caused bad feelings with Silverman. Johnny Carson was reworking his contract just as Michaels' came up for renewal. NBC focused on Carson.

Michaels' manager, Bernie Brillstein, says he was looking for an excuse to quit. When negotiations went sour, they bailed. Michaels said that for him to return, "They would have had to make me feel special, and they didn't."

At the final show of the fifth season aired, the camera focused on the "On-air" light outside studio 8H. The light flickered and went dark. That left a question about the show's future.

After the show, Jane Curtin said, "I will not set foot here again."

In his own gesture, Michaels gave out cigarette lighters with the inscription: "Nice working with you . . . 1975-1980."

NBC gave up on Michaels, but they still owned *Saturday Night Live*. Silverman was determined to see his one success continue. Several new producers were considered before the network settled on Michaels' former associate producer, Jean Doumanian.

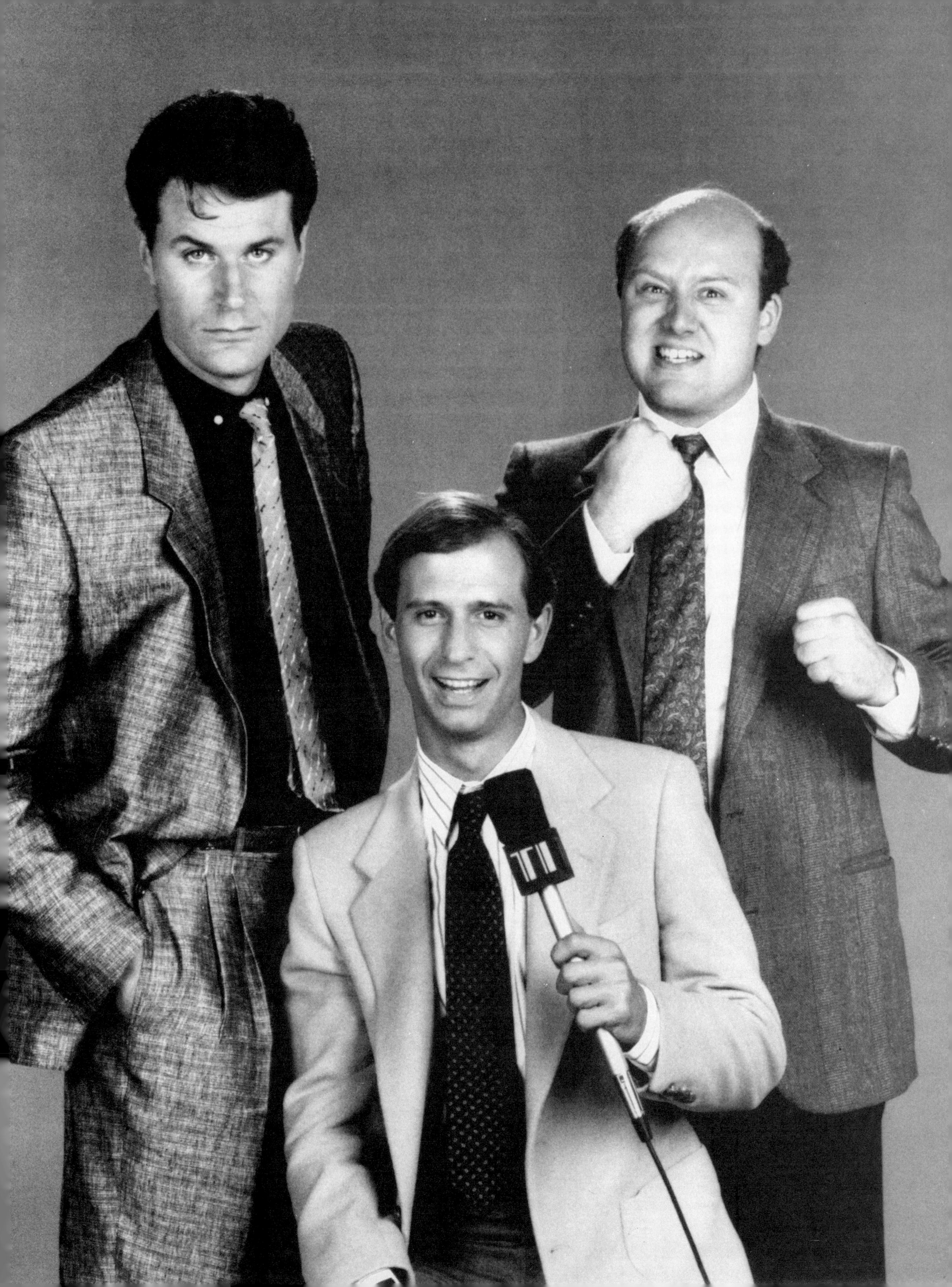

XIV

NOT READY FOR ANY TIME

Lorne Michaels was ambivalent about coming back for a 6th year in 1980. His cast would be gone and he'ld have to start from scratch.

He was just too tired.

Your children will eat you

Years later, he explained his decision, saying, "Fellini said that when you're making a picture, the director is like a father. Everybody—the actors, the actresses, the designers—eats at one big table every day. They're like the children. 'But the moment the picture is over,' he said, 'you must leave the picture. Or, the children, they will eat you.'

"I kept from being eaten by leaving. Worse, *Saturday Night Live* began to be perceived as a step, not an end. It changed the attitude of the people who worked there. I was trying to hold the show together. It was all I cared about. It gave me all I needed, used all my talent, all my energy. But for others, it was time to move on."

> *Newsday called it "offensive and raunchy." Another simply said, "Vile from New York, it's Saturday Night." Writer Barry Blaustein noted, "You realized that the whole world unanimously hated you."*

Silverman kept the corpse alive

NBC wasn't going to let *SNL* die. In the ratings wasteland, *Saturday Night Live* was all they had going for them.

NBC owned the show. When Michaels quit, they hunted for a new producer.

Michaels wanted Franken and Davis to rise to the throne, but after Franken's "Limo for a Lamo" attack on Silverman, he was out. The network wanted the show to have continuity with the original hit. They hired Jean Doumanian as Michaels' replacement.

A friend of Woody Allen's, she had been an associate producer for Michaels. Few believed she was up to the job.

When veteran *SNL* writer Herb Sargent heard the news, he congratulated her and added, "You're crazy!" Even Michaels had no confidence in her.

She may be classy, but she's no Lorne Michaels

Doumanian lacked Michaels' go-for-the-jugular comedy sense. She was a conservative businesswoman. Where drugs had been commonplace in the past, she banned them and distributed anti- drug pamphlets to her employees.

Veteran writers and production assistants, weighed their options, and deserted at the announcement of Doumanian as producer. The continuity NBC wanted would be tenuous.

Veteran director Dave Wilson and associate producer Audrey Dickman stayed. Michaels' younger cousin, Neil Levy, was hired as talent coordinator.

Isolated by a circles of friends

Michaels had had his own core circle. Now Doumanian created hers. She used them to insulate herself from the world.

This inner circle included Letty Aronson, Woody Allen's sister. And Mary Pat Kelly, the sister of Bill Murray's girlfriend.

Doumanian hired writers from diverse backgrounds. David Sheffield came from an advertising job in Mississippi; Sean Kelly from *National Lampoon*. Another had been a producer on *The Mike Douglas Show*.

The new producer followed her predecessor's lead, hunting for talent in comedy clubs. She wanted to build her own repertory company with, Doumanian said, "the look of the Eighties."

Building the new company

She narrowed her pool of applicants. An early choice was Joe Piscopo. He performed memorable characters in stand-up, but had also starred in a stinker of an NBC series called *A Dog's Life*. The hyper, off-center Gilbert Gottfried was another early choice.

Doumanian was looking for strong women. Gail Matthius was an early practitioner of "Valley-girl" humor; Ann Risley yet another connection to Woody Allen. (Risley was in Allen's *Annie Hall*, *Manhattan*, and *Stardust Memories*.) Denny Dillon was a short blonde comedian who had appeared on a show during Michaels' early years.

Doumanian's chosen "star"—picked to be her next Chevy Chase—was Charles Rocket. Rocket had come to comedy from television journalism. He was a reporter for a local news broadcast in which he did his "Rocket Report", man-on-the-street thing.

Tartikoff called Rocket a hybrid of Bill Murray and Chevy Chase. He took it as a compliment, but it was a ghost of *Saturday Night*'s past.

Doumanian fills her Black quota

All Doumanian's selections were lily white. She set up auditions to find a black *SNL* cast member.

A 19-year-old kid from Roosevelt, New York campaigned for the spot. He had already made the rounds of comedy clubs for the past four years. A "Gonzo"-style comic like Belushi, he owed even more to Richard Pryor.

The young, Black comedian showed up at *SNL* and performed for anyone and everyone. He quickly won staff people over, and later recalled he auditioned six times.

Doumanian, not understanding the out-of-control humor, was slow to buy the new cast member. At last, she relented and let the comedian in, not as a cast member, but as a "featured player."

Doumanian's featured players were hardly better than extras. Such was Eddie Murphy's introduction to *Saturday Night Live*.

Trouble on Saturday night

Trouble began to brew as soon as production began. The cast and writers were full of the mythology. They felt charmed. In the words of one, they had "an attitude of presumptive arrogance."

A line, never seen before on *SNL*, was drawn between cast and writers. The writers deemed the cast, "awful, hopeless."

Doumanian fostered negative feelings. The communal days were gone. Michaels had always worked closely with writers; Doumanian wasn't nearly so helpful.

"Make it funnier," she would write on a weak script, leaving the writer to shake his head in wonder. One writer said, "Jean was not an intellectual."

Doumanian seemed insecure in this new environment she didn't fully understand. Insecurity bred over-control.

Neil Levy said Doumanian had the "inability to accept her inabilities." A journalist at *Newsday* called Doumanian "conservative, insecure, inexperienced, unadventurous."

The debut falls flat

Writer David Sheffield was a late arrival. When he landed in New York, he said he found an "air of doom" hanging over the show.

Sheffield was right. Doumanian's debut was universally panned as full of cheap sex jokes with no point. In one case, Ann Risley played Rosalynn Carter the day after Jimmy, played by Joe Piscopo, lost the election. The joke revolved around Rosalynn unbuttoning her blouse wanting Jimmy to make love to her on the Oval Office desk now that the fate of the nation no longer rested on him.

Another sketch portrayed a gay Army unit stationed at Fort Dix. Their marching call: "I won't go down on anyone, Uncle Sam's the only one."

The critics ravage the show

Newsday called it "offensive and raunchy." Another simply said, "Vile from New York, it's Saturday

Night." Writer Barry Blaustein noted, "You realized that the whole world unanimously hated you."

Doumanian was horrified. She held a staff meeting the following Monday.

Unlike Michaels' supportive meetings, one writer called Doumanian's session "a huge cat fight."

She played a tape of the first show and said, "Watch this. And I hope you hate it, because you wrote it."

It only got worse

SNL continued on its precipitous decline. Weekend Update featured Denny Dillon as a dominatrix weatherlady with Charles Rocket hanging on the weathermap in leather. Dillon tortured Rocket as she did the nation's weather.

That humor typified the show. Brandon Tartikoff later said he was "crazed" and "appalled" by what he saw.

Doumanian wasn't even good for business. Her debut show lost five million viewers. Her second show lost 3.4 million more. Advertising plummeted.

SNL lost half its client base. Thirty second spots that sold for $50,000 in Michaels' show went for $25,000 under Doumanian.

NBC president Fred Silverman wasn't fond of the show when it was his only money-maker. Now he hated it. Tartikoff said that watching *SNL* failing "drove Fred nuts."

Silverman frequently said of Doumanian, "Get rid of her. We've got to do something."

Tartikoff hung in a while longer.

One small candle in the darkness

In the midst of failure, one bright spot slowly emerged. Eddie Murphy had done very little for the first few Doumanian shows. "She tried to 'Garrett Morris' me," Murphy later said, "turn me into the little token nigger." He would begin to play a larger role.

The writing team of Blaistein and Sheffield wanted to write something in Weekend Update about a judge in Cleveland who instituted a quota of a minimum of two white players on a basketball team. Murphy created the character of basketball player Raheem Abdul Muhammed for the skit.

He editorialized the classic line, "I mean, we ain't got much, at least let us have basketball." Murphy got the only laugh all night.

Murphy came back more regularly on Weekend Update. He launched a barbed attack on his black predecessor, Garrett Morris. "If I get drafted," Murphy pointed out, "who's going to be 'The Black Guy' on *Saturday Night Live*? You want a tough soldier? You want a guy whose very name scares the very hell out of me?" Murphy holds up a picture of Morris. "Here's your man. He may be overage, but he's got a lot of free time."

Murphy began to do his stand-up act when time needed to be filled. He was a spark in a lifeless corpse.

The suits get involved

Doumanian didn't know what was funny. It scared the brass, so execs began to take a more active creative role.

They attended read-throughs and rehearsals. In many cases, they decided which skits went on."There were," one production assistant remembered, "blue suits everywhere."

Lorne Michaels had fought the suits from the start and won. Now the "blue suits" were running the show.

Rocket makes them see red

In the darkest hours, it was Doumanian's "next Chevy Chase", Charles Rocket, who sealed the fate of the show. Charlene Tilton of *Dallas* was the host that week.

The country was gripped in "Who shot J.R.?" fever. In a parody attempt, cast members tried to kill Rocket.

At the end, Rocket was shot. When it came time for goodnights, he was on stage with Tilton and the rest, in a wheelchair and wearing a head bandage.

Tilton asked him how he felt. Rocket replied, "Oh, man, it's the first time I've been shot in my life. I'd like to know who the fuck did it."

Tilton gasped.

The other cast members giggled.

It took a split second for everyone in the control room to realize Rocket had said "fuck" on the air. Director Dave Wilson stormed out, saying, "That's the end of live television."

The brass go livid and heads roll

Silverman saw it at home and went into orbit. Rocket barely remembered saying the word.

He hadn't planned to. He explained his mistake to Doumanian.

Rocket and Doumanian apologized to the major brass, but Doumanian warned that if Rocket was canned, she'd go to. That didn't bother a soul.

Brandon Tartikoff called Jean Doumanian into his office during the week and told her she was out. It wasn't just the Rocket incident, it was her entire performance. NBC just couldn't sacrifice *Saturday Night Live*.

When she went back to her office, she made the announcement. The afternoon was very emotional. Doumanian delivered a speech and told her staff and cast to "carry on in the *Saturday Night* tradition."

Many would. But not Rocket. He, too, was axed.

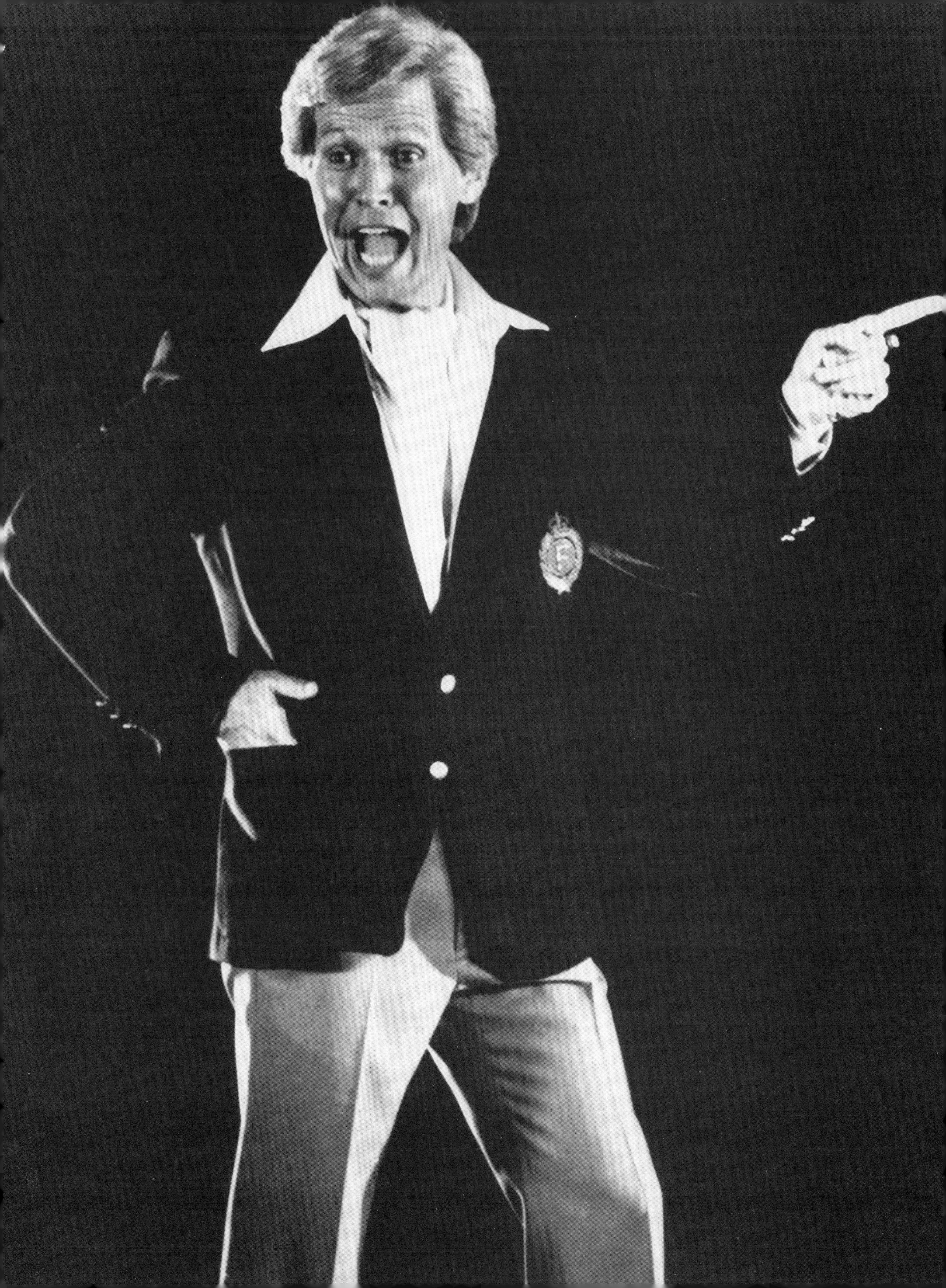

XV. A CORPORATE VIKING FUNERAL

Dick Ebersol is the young network exec who teamed with Lorne Michaels in 1975 to create *Saturday Night*. Now Brandon Tartikoff would convince him to return as producer.

Ebersol emphasized his original connection with the show in his introductory speech, saying, "This show, or at least the general form, was borne out of me as much as anyone in the whole world."

Cleaning out the dead wood and looking for new directions

Ebersol wanted continuity with the Michaels era. He called everyone he knew from the original show.

> *Ebersol emphasized his original connection with the show in his introductory speech, saying, "This show, or at least the general form, was borne out of me as much as anyone in the whole world."*

"The idea was merchandising how the show was going to be perceived," Ebersol explained. John Belushi offered advice, but little substantial support. His wife, Judy, however, came aboard as a writer.

Ebersol immediately removed Doumanian's inner circle, and a few of the writers and actors—Gilbert Gottfried and Ann Risley, as well as Rocket. He would have dropped Denny Dillon, but his budget wouldn't support it.

Ebersol replaced the fired cast members with Tim Kazurinsky— a Belushi recommendation. He also set his sights on players from SCTV in Canada, hiring Tony Rosato. Soon afterward, he brought in Robin Duke.

Still, Ebersol craved "continuity." Franken and Davis agreed to host Ebersol's second show.

The ideal premiere host fell into his lap one day. Chevy Chase dropped by just to say "hi," and Ebersol begged him to host his first show. Chase agreed.

Returning Saturday Night Live to its roots

Ebersol contacted Lorne Michaels. Michaels suggested that Ebersol hire a prominent creative mind from the original show, Michael O'Donoghue.

When Ebersol met O'Donoghue, the writer was still wary of television. He felt *SNL* was doomed.

O'Donoghue said he wanted the show to go out in a blaze of glory. He wanted to give the show "a decent Viking funeral."

Ebersol let the attitude slide. He offered O'Donoghue lots of money, and O'Donoghue accepted.

"TV money is hard to turn down," O'Donoghue later said. "It's the purest of motives."

The highly eccentric O'Donoghue insisted his title be either "Reich Marshall" or "Godhead", but settled for Chief of Staff. He was brutally honest when he met the cast.

He told them, "Everybody on this show sucks, except for Murphy. But everybody else, you do nothing for me."

O'Donoghue was disgusted by the corporate atmosphere. He ordered his staff to create graffiti on the walls. He said to "Make this place look like a comedy office!"

On the right track again

The Chevy Chase premiere went a long way to repair the show. The New York *Times* called the show "watchable" again. *Newsday* said it was "better tasting and better written."

The momentum soon stalled when the writers went on strike. NBC put the show on hiatus, but renewed it for another year.

Franken and Davis were never called to host. Tony Rosato didn't last.

As the show began to pick up steam again, Ebersol and O'Donoghue took opposite approaches. O'Donoghue wanted to fill a dying series with twisted humor; Ebersol craved slick commercial product.

Younger viewers began tuning in, so Ebersol tailored the show toward them. He wanted rock-video length skits, quick and simple gags, and nothing too complex. Ebersol frowned on political satire, a traditional *SNL* staple, because he felt kids weren't interested.

While the cat's away....

Ebersol was in California courting actress Susan St. James. O'Donoghue created gory sketches for the Halloween show: the Reagans hack Jane Fonda apart and eat her for dinner; host Donald Pleasance has dinner with a young lady and keeps pouring wine, the camera reveals to actually be blood coming from an intravenous tube in his young dinner companion.

Ebersol was appalled. None of the skits were aired.

O'Donoghue and Ebersol's relationship became more strained. "Dick could fire me," O'Donoghue said. "I couldn't fire him."

O'Donoghue kept berating his staff and actors. Eventually Ebersol fired him.

The show goes on

The show was renewed for another year. Without O'Donoghue, the corporate atmosphere returned. One production assistant said, "With Dick things run more smoothly, although it borders on dull."

Robin Duke left. Actress Christine Ebersole came and went. Julia Louis-Dreyfus, Brad Hall, and Gary Kroeger came aboard.

Eddie Murphy and Joe Piscopo emerged as the stars. Piscopo made waves, especially with his impersonations of Frank Sinatra.

He identified with Sinatra so heavily that he spoke in Sinatra's voice off-camera. He teamed up with Murphy both on- and off-stage.

Murphy became the more important personality. His first movie, *48 Hours,* was a huge hit. The Chevy Chase/John Belushi/Bill Murray syndrome struck again. Ebersol was quick to downplay the ensemble to focus on his star.

Belushi's younger brother, Jim, joined the cast during the '83 season. He proved just as volatile as his brother had been. Belushi railed against the turn away from ensemble and threatened to quit. Kazurinsky brought him back to earth, telling him to "Get off the fucking cross."

Prepackaged fun, without the surprises

The 1984 season would be Murphy's last. The show had become a consistent commercial success, but sacrificed much of the zest. Increasingly *Saturday Night* wasn't live anymore.

Ebersole increasingly pre-taped. Even the band was put on tape. Almost half a given show was taped.

1984 provided one experiment, In the short run, it pushed the show to new heights. In the end, it caused problems.

In the past, when cast slots needed to be filled, "enlightened amateurs", as Lorne Michaels had called them, were hired. Now Ebersol brought in established professionals Billy Crystal and Martin Short.

They were both immediate hits. Crystal's Fernando character created a national sensation with the phrase: "You look mahlevous!" Short was equally successful with his Ed Grimley character.

After one season, both Crystal and Short left, leaving a gaping hole to fill. Rather than deal with the hole, Ebersol resigned to pursue his series of professional wrestling specials.

He had married St. James and begun a family. He wanted to spend more time with them.

Once more NBC had to find a new producer.

Meanwhile, what was Lorne Micheals doing?

Lorne Michaels didn't cut all ties to NBC when he walked out on *SNL*. He put together a show based on the same formula.

Although would be taped, Michaels wanted it shot in front of a live audience in one take as if live. He wanted to call it *Friday Night*, but settled on *The New Show*. Michaels brought in many of the writers from his five years on *SNL*, including Tom Davis and Al Franken.

The New Show had to live up to its name. Somehow, something had to be *new*; different from *Saturday Night Live*. Michaels said, "I always thought on *Saturday Night* we were just trying to be funny. But quite often the subject matter we were trying to be funny about hadn't been dealt with on television. This time, we aren't going to have the advantage of being new. You can't fake virginity."

The show died trying to find its identity. Michaels didn't understand the sensibilities of prime time.

In an attempt to save his new series, Michaels convinced Dick Ebersol to let him work on familiar territory and use 8H when *Saturday Night* wasn't there. Nothing helped.

Buck Henry of *The New Show* cast said, "There were an enormous number of people waiting for Lorne to fail."

Michaels' failure exorcised a ghost at *SNL*. When Michaels' series was canceled, one of the post-Michaels *Saturday Night* producers said, "Everybody here took a deep breath and said, 'We're legitimate.'"

Eventually Michaels and his original brainchild, SNL, would be reunited. A deal was hammered out between NBC and Michaels. He would return as *Saturday Night*'s producer ten years after he first created it.

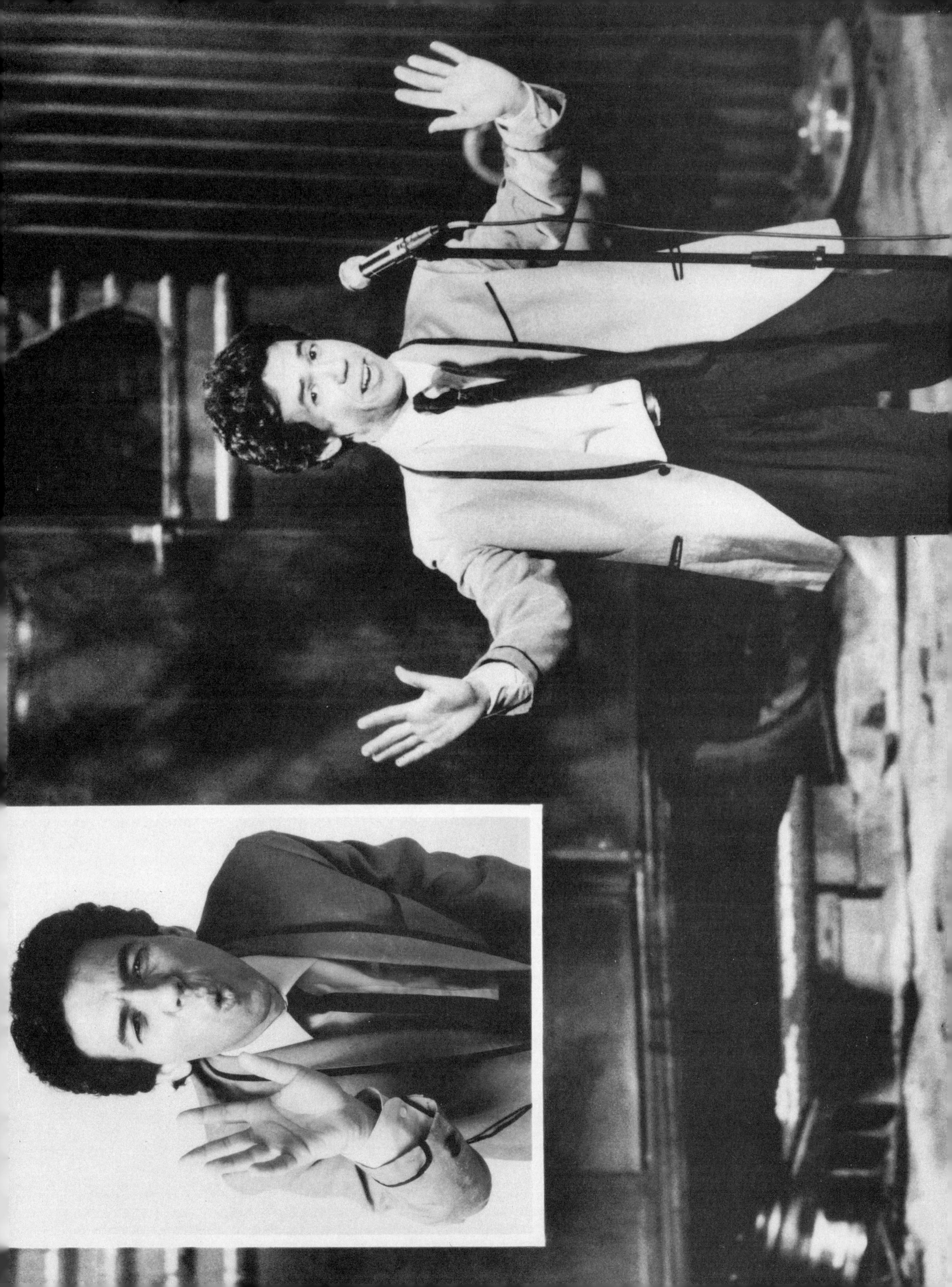

XVI THE FUTURE OF SATURDAY NIGHT LIVE

Michaels' original *Saturday Night* had been startlingly new and innovative; the new series simply offered quality comedy. Old faces returned, including Franken and Davis. Davis said the new *SNL* would "maintain the integrity of the engine."

Michaels felt the show needed to be spruced up with fresh and energetic people. That the show had lost the ensemble feeling.

He brought in a mix of newcomers and well-known actors to fill the repertory company. Joan Cusack, Robert Downey, Jr., Anthony Michael Hall, Terry Sweeney, Randy Quaid, Danitra Vance, Damon Wayans, Nora Dunn, and Jon Lovitz all joined *SNL* that year.

Michaels fights to keep SNL on the air

The show began to improve almost immediately, but it was still shaky. "I made some whopper mistakes," Michaels said of his first year back. "But having been through the pounding and the body blows of *The New Show*, and then the stuff I had gone

> "We're a comedy show, not a civil-liberties forum. Our job is to be funny and bright."
>
> In 1991, Saturday Night Live won a Peabody Award for being a television "institution." It's an interesting place for this once anti-Establishment rebel. Former SNL cast member Gilbert Gottfried may have said it best: "Saturday Night Live has gone beyond being funny or unfunny. Now it's a restaurant in a good location."

through in my personal life, my instinct was to hang on. I thought, 'It gets very bad, and then it has to get better.'

"I had to rebuild the writing staff, which was very difficult to do. I had to lure back the designers. The band, for fuck's sake, which had been the heart of the show, wasn't even on camera anymore. I decided I couldn't do it all in one season, but since I believed as I did in 1975—that this thing had value and is important—then it was worth doing.

"But Brandon [Tartikoff of NBC] still canceled the show at the end of the 1985 season. I flew to California and said, 'I know I can turn this thing around. I know how to do it. I know what needs to be done.'"

It was the same non-specific, gut-level approach Michaels had used ten years earlier. And it worked. *SNL* was given one more year.

Michaels shuffled the deck, changing the cast again. This time magic struck. Lovitz and Dunn returned for the '86-'87 season, joining Dana Carvey, Phil Hartman, Jan Hooks, Victoria Jackson, and Dennis Miller.

Miller took the Weekend Update anchor slot, ending each with "That's the news and I'm outta here!". His off-beat, hip style made him the most popular Weekend Update anchor since Chevy Chase originated the sketch.

Chase himself said, "I thought this was the best guy to do it since I did it. But the problem with it, I felt, is that he was playing for an audience rather than making it appear to really be a serious news show—that's when it got really big laughs, in my opinion."

Memorable characters such as the Pathological Liar, Master Thespian, and the Church Lady all took hold that year. *SNL* began its slow climb back.

The show regained footing as each year passed. Kevin Nealon joined the following year and was made a full cast member for '87-'88.

The fifteenth anniversary special

Saturday Night Live celebrated a triumphant fifteen years in a prime time special. Cast members from the entire span of the series returned, even a few from the Dick Ebersol period. Dan Aykroyd, Chevy Chase, Steve Martin, Laraine Newman, Jane Curtin, Christopher Guest, and Martin Short all made appearances.

Like most retrospectives, there was an emphasis on taped material from the past. On the other hand, Paul Simon and Prince presented new musical numbers.

The special garnered the show's highest ratings ever. It told the world Saturday *Night Live* was back.

Michaels recalled, "Sometime around the fifteenth-anniversary show I thought, 'Hey, maybe I *did* do something. All I want is to do the show as long as I can, where the curve is still going up, where it's getting better."

Tainted with tragedy

The fifteenth year was tainted by tragedy. Gilda Radner died of ovarian cancer the Saturday of the final show aired. She was the second original Not Ready for Prime Time player to die.

That evening host Steve Martin included a tribute to Radner. "I was awakened at a quarter to nine on a show day," Michaels remembered, "and it was CBS News, saying, 'Gilda Radner's dead, do you have any comment?'

"That night, Steve Martin hosted the show. We showed the piece that he and Gilda had done to 'Dancing in the Dark'. I worked with him on a line to say after the tape. I don't think I've ever seen him that shaken, that moved. And we were pros. We were in the middle of a comedy show.

"I knew Gilda was sick, but when I talked to her, she didn't give me that impression. She was fighting it. I tended to buy into the hope she talked about. People older than I, to whom I talked, were more pessimistic. We were closer to brother and sister than any other relationship on the show."

Again, the show moves on

Another Canadian, Mike Myers joined the show in the '89 season. He brought his popular character, Wayne Campbell, the host of the public-access cable show *Wayne's World*. Dana Carvey became his sidekick, Garth.

The film, *Wayne's World*, finally brought *SNL* to the big screen. It grossed more than $100 million at the box office.

Stability evolved on the show. "I signed a four-year contract last year," said Michaels, "which was my way of reassuring the network of my commitment to the series."

Still, not all is static. Cast members still leave for greener pastures, some cordially, some not. Jon Lovitz left after the 1990 season.

"Jon left because, in many ways, he was unhappy," revealed Michaels, "he didn't feel he was being treated with respect . . . by the writers."

Jan Hooks defected at the end of the 1991 season. "I hadn't expected Jan to leave," Michaels said. "I thought she was coming back, but then she got the opportunity to do *Designing Women*. It left a big hole. Now, whether or not *Designing Women* shows her off in the same way we showed her off, who knows?"

Dennis Miller was the other notable departure at the end of '91. He started his own late-night talk show, which lasted seven months against stiff competition before it was canceled.

Departures aren't the blow they once were. Michaels said, "Now, I would hate it if Phil Hartman left. Phil has done more work that's touched greatness than probably anyone else who's ever been there. Would he be paid more if he were Jay Leno's sidekick? Of course. There are thirty or forty jobs that would pay him more."

Still some excitement in the old rebel after all

Egos played an important factor in *SNL* in the past. There hasn't been anything to rival the infamous Chevy Chase-Bill Murray backstage brawl since, but there have been points of contention. Nora Dunn's walkout on the show hosted by controversial comedian Andrew Dice Clay was one of the hotter points.

"The true story is told from many perspectives," said Michaels. "Clay had just sold out Madison Square Garden, which, for a one-man show, seemed to me like something was happening there. I knew that his act was coarse. I'd encountered a diversity of opinion on him: from funny to offensive.

"I had no problem with people not liking Clay's comedy, but what I was so astonished by—particularly in the press—was that we were criticized for putting him on television in the first place. Clay didn't deserve the treatment he got, even though there was some validity to Nora's position. I also think she was coming to the end of her time on the show and was going through a big emotional upheaval about deciding to leave or not. She was going back and forth about it. There are certain people who have to break things off and make it so they can't go back, for fear they will go back. Lots of people break off relationships that way.

"We're a comedy show, not a civil-liberties forum. Our job is to be funny and bright."

In 1991, *Saturday Night Live* won a Peabody Award for being a television "institution." It's an interesting place for this once anti-Establishment rebel. Former *SNL* cast member Gilbert Gottfried may have said it best: "*Saturday Night Live* has gone beyond being funny or unfunny. Now it's a restaurant in a good location."

Maybe Lorne Michaels was wrong about success, after all.

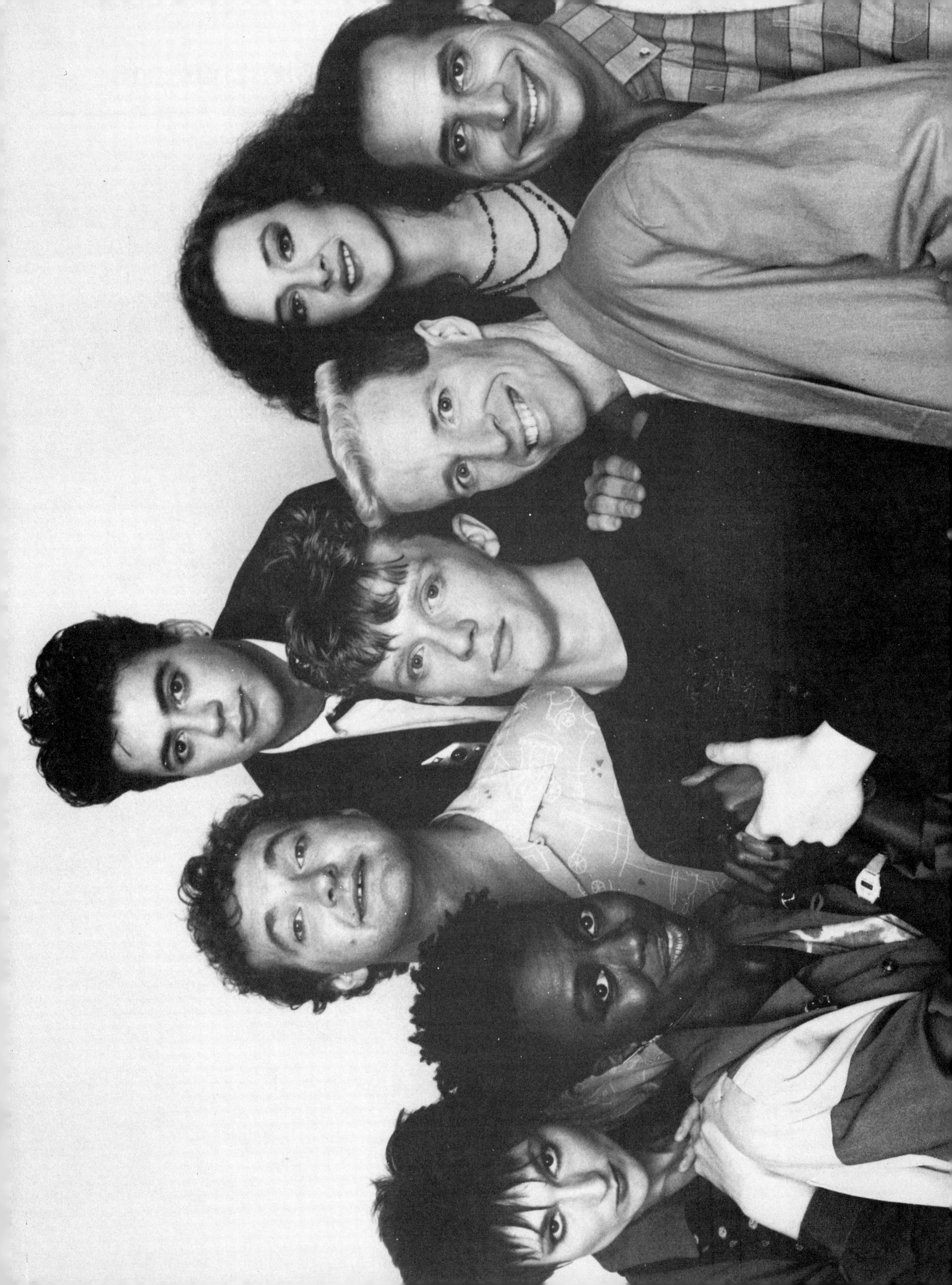

THE PLAYERS

Dan Akroyd

1975-'80 seasons

Born in Ottawa, Dan Akroyd was a founding "Not Ready for Prime Time" Player. His characters included Beldar Conehead, one of two "wild and crazy guys", Blues Brother Elwood Jake, and a string of impersonations. His sketches included the Super Bass-O-Matic, French Chef Julia Child, and the Point/Counterpoint segment of Weekend Update.

Before *SNL*, Belushi was with the Second City improv troupe and appeared on *Coming Up Rosie* for CBC TV. After leaving *SNL*, he appeared in a number of popular films. Akroyd was nominated for an Oscar for *Driving Miss Daisy*, and is a part owner of the Hard Rock Cafe in New York.

Films include: *1941, The Blues Brothers, Ghostbusters, Doctor Detroit, Ghostbusters II, Driving Miss Daisy, Nothing But Trouble, Spies Like Us*

James Belushi

1983-'85 seasons

Brother of the late John Belushi.

Member of the Second City improv group for two years.

Films include: *Salvador, About Last Night, Red Heat, K-9, Only the Lonely.*

John Belushi

1975-'79 seasons

A Chicagoan, John Belushi enjoyed a remarkable career before dying of a drug overdose. Cathy Evelyn Smith pleaded gulty to involuntary manslaughter.

Belushi's most famous *SNL* skits included the Bees, Samurai, The Blues Brothers, and various impersonations. Before *SNL*, Belushi was with the Second City improv troupe and performed for the *National Lampoon Radio Hour*. After leaving *SNL*, he starred in a series of movies.

Films include: *Animal House, Old Boyfriends, 1941, Goin' South, The Blues Brothers, Neighbors*

Chevy Chase

1975-'76 season

Cornelius Crane, later known as Chevy Chase, was born in New York City. He worked as both writer and performer fo SNL, winning an Emmy for best supporting player.

His words, "I'm Chevy Chase, and you're not" became famous as the opening lines for Weekend Update. Famous Chase sketches included Mr. Spock, a sportscaster for The Claudine Longet Invitational Ski Tournament, and President Ford.

Before SNL, Chase was one of National Lampoon's Lemmings, wrote for Alan King and the Smothers Brothers, performed for the National Lampoon Radio Hour, and appeared in the movie The Groove Tube. After leaving, he made films.

Films include: National Lampoon Vacation, Caddyshack, Oh Heavenly Dog!, Under the Rainbow, Fletch, Three Amigos, Spies Like Us, Perfect, Memoirs of an Invisible Man

Billy Crystal

1984-'85 season

A native New Yorker, Crystal was already a success before joining SNL. He had co-starred in *Soap* . He joined Robin Williams and Whoopi Goldberg for *Comic Relief* a series of specials to raise money for the homeless. Crystal won a 1992 Emmy Award. His most memorable *Saturday Night* character was Fernando.

Films include: *Throw Mamma From the Train*, *When Harry Met Sally*, *City Slickers*.

Jane Curtin

1975-'80 seasons

Born in Cambridge, Jane Curtin was an original "Not Ready for Prime Time" Player. Famous characters included Fris de Flamino, Rula Lenska, her part in the Point/Counterpoint segment of Weekend Update, and an impersonation of Eleanor Roosevelt. Before *SNL*, Curtin was a member of The Proposition improv troupe, performed "The Last of the Red Hot Lovers", and both created and performed for "Pretzels". After leaving *SNL*, she played Allie for *Kate and Allie*, winning two Emmys and starred in TV's *Working It Out*, but the series was cancelled in its first season.

Joan Cusack

1985-'86 season

Born in Evanston IL, Joan Cusack graduated from the University of Wisconsin with an English degree. She made her debut in the feature *My Bodyguard*. She was nominated for an Oscar for her role in *Working Girl.*.

Films include: *My Bodyguard.,Say Anything, Broadcast News, Sixteen Candles, Working Girl..*

Denny Dillon

1980-'81 season

Denny Dillon was born in Cleveland, OH and got her degree from Syracuse University. She appeared on Broadway in *The Skin of Our Teeth*, *Gypsy*, and received a Tony nomination for *My One and Only*. SHe currently stars on the HBO series *Dream On*. Her television guest appearances include *Night Court*, *Designing Women*, and *Miami Vice*.

126 SNL! THE STORY OF SATURDAY NIGHT

Robert Downey, Jr.

1985-'86 season

A native New Yorker, Downey is the son of avant-garde filmmaker Robert Downey, Sr. His career began at the age of 5 in the film *Pound*. He will soon appear in Sir Richard Attenborough's film *Charlie*.

Films include: *Pound, First Born, Weird Science, Less Than Zero*.

Julia Louis-Dreyfus

1982-'85 seasons

Now Elaine on NBC's *Seinfeld*, Louis-Dreyfus married fellow *SNL* cast member Brad Hall, and starred with him in *Trolls*. She has worked as a writer, including for *SNL*. The actress received her training at the BS Program at Northwestern University.

Films include: *National Lampoon's Christmas Vacation, Soul Man, Hannah and Her Sisters, Trolls*.

Mary Gross

1981-'85 seasons

Mary Gross was born in Chicago, the sister of *Family Ties* star Michael Gross. She got her break on *SNL* after being spotted by Dick Ebersol while a member of Chicago's Second City troupe.

Films include: *Club Paradise*, *Hot to Trot*, *Casual Sex*.

Anthony Michael Hall

1985-'86 season

Born in Boston, Hall began his acting career doing television commercials at the age of 8.

Films include: *Sixteen Candles, The Breakfast Club, Weird Science, Johnny Be Good., Vacation, Edward Scissorhands.*

Rich Hall

1984-'85 season

Rich Hall grew up in Charlotte, NC. He began his career in stand-up in nightclubs. David Letterman discovered him at the Improvisation in New York. Letterman gave Hall a writing job on his show. His other television credits include *Friday's* and *Not Necessarily the News*. He also wrote the popular books *Sniglets*, *More Sniglets*, and *Unexplained Sniglets of the Universe*.

Jan Hooks

1985-'91 seasons

Now on *Designing Women*, for *SNL* Hooks was noted for impressions, including Nancy Reagan, Kitty Dukakis, Tammy Faye Baker, and Diane Sawyer. She won a regional Emmy for *Tush* and appeared on *Comedy Break, The Half-Hour Comedy Hour*, and *The Joe Piscopo Special*. Hooks is a native of Atlanta, attended the University of West Florida, but returned to appear in dinner theater and the Off Peachtree Theatre.

Films include: *Pee-Wee's Big Adventure, Wildcats, Batman Returns*.

Tim Kazurinsky

1981-'84 seasons

Kazurinsky was born in Pennsylvania, but grew up in Australia. He returned to the States and joined the Chicago Second City group from 1978-1980. He co-wrote the film *My Bodyguard*. and the Molly Ringwald film *For Keeps*.

Films include: the string of *Police Academy*'s

Jon Lovitz
1984-'90 season

Jon Lovitz received a BAmin drama from the University of California at Irvine. He began classes with The Groundlings, then joined their Sunday Company. Twice nominated for an Emmy on *Saturday Night Live*, Lovitz's characters spawned well-recognized popular phrases such as "Yeah, that's the ticket!" and "I gotta go...I gotta go!"

Films include: *A League of Their Own, Jumping Jack Flash, The Three Amigos, Big*

Dennis Miller

1985-'91 seasons

His syndicated late-night talk show canceled after 7 months, Dennis Miller is best remembered as a Weekend Update anchor. A native of Pittsburgh, he graduated from Point Park College with a major in journalism and began working as a stand-up comedian in clubs in his hometown in 1977.

After three years, Miller got his break in New York at Catch a Rising Star and The Comic Strip. He returned to Pittsburgh for the local *PM Magazine* television show. Before joining *SNL*, he won a Gabriel Award for hosting *Punchline*, a children's television show.

SNL! THE STORY OF SATURDAY NIGHT LIVE

Eddie Murphy

1980-'84 seasons

Several of Eddie Murphy's characters for *SNL* became hits, including Buckwheat and Mr. Robinson, the spoof of children's television's Mr. Rogers. Murphy has starred in a number of movies and became a successful singer with the hit, "Party All the Time". Murphy is scheduled to appear in a third *Beverly Hills Cop* picture.

Films include *48 Hours, Another 48 Hours, Beverly Hills Cop 1, Beverly Hills Cop 2, Coming To America, Trading Places, Boomerang*

Bill Murray

1977-'80 seasons

Bill Murray was born in Evanston, Illinois, and hired to replace Chevy Chase on *SNL*. Bill Murray's most famous characters included Nick the lounge singer, Todd Di LaMuca of the Nerds, and movie critic and gossip columnist for Weekend Update.

Murray was romantically involved with Gilda Radner but married Mickey Kelly. He engaged in a backstage fistfight with Chevy Chase.

Before *SNL*, Murray was a member of Second City, wrote for *National Lampoon*, and appeared on Howard Cosell's *Saturday Night Live*. After *SNL*, he appeared in films.

Films include: *Meatballs, Caddyshack, Stripes, Where the Buffalo Roam, Ghostbusters, Razor's Edge, Ghostbusters II, What About Bob*

Larraine Newman

1975-'80 seasons

Born in LA, Larraine Newman became one of the original "Not Ready for Prime Time" Players. Her characters included Connie Conehead, rock critic Z. Jones for Weekend Update, Sheri the stewardess for the Godfather Group Therapy sketch, and an impersonation of Barbara Streisand.

Before *SNL*, Newman was with The Groundlings improv troupe and performed for TV specials with Lily Tomlin produced by Lorne Michaels. After leaving *SNL*, she co-headlined a 1979 TV special.

Films include: *American Hot Wax*

Gilda Radner

1975-'80 seasons

Born in Detroit, Gilda Radner became a founding member of the "Not Ready for Prime Time" Players. She won an Emmy in 1977 for best leading actress. Lorne Michaels launched her in *Gilda Live from New York* and NBC wanted to give her a series.

Famous characters included Baba Wawa, Miss Emily Litella ("Never mind!"), Roseanne Roseanadanna ("It's *alll*-ways *some*thing, if it's not one thing . . . it's another."), and one of the girls in the Uncle Roy sketches. Before *SNL*, Radner was a member of Toronto's Second City and performed for the *National Lampoon Radio Hour* and the *National Lampoon Show*. After leaving *SNL*, she appeared in films.

Radner was romantically involved with Bill Murray.

Films include: *Gilda Live from New York, The Last Detail, First Family, Hanky Panky, The Woman in Red, Haunted Honeymoon*

Martin Short

Martin Short, a native Canadian, joined the Toronto company of Second City and won an Emmy for his work on *SCTV*. Short has appeared in many comedy specials. He is probably best known for his SNL character, Ed Grimley.

Films include: *Three Amigos, Innerspace, Father of the Bride*.

Pamela Stephenson

1984-'85 season

Pamela Stephenson was born in New Zealand and grew up in Sydney, Australia. She starred in the British television hit, *Not the Nine O'Clock News*. Stephenson appeared in London as Mabel in *The Pirates of Penzance* . She married to Scottish comedian Billy Connolly and lives in Los Angeles with their children.

Films include:*Superman III, Finder's Keeper's , The Secret Policeman's Other Ball.*

Terry Sweeney

1985-'86 season

Terry Sweeney was born in St. Alban's, NY. He developed his interest in comedy while working at a drug rehabilitation center as a counselor. Since leaving *SNL*, Sweeney has toured with his one-man show as Nancy Reagan in *It's Still My Turn*. He co-wrote the movies *Shag* and *Loose Women*.

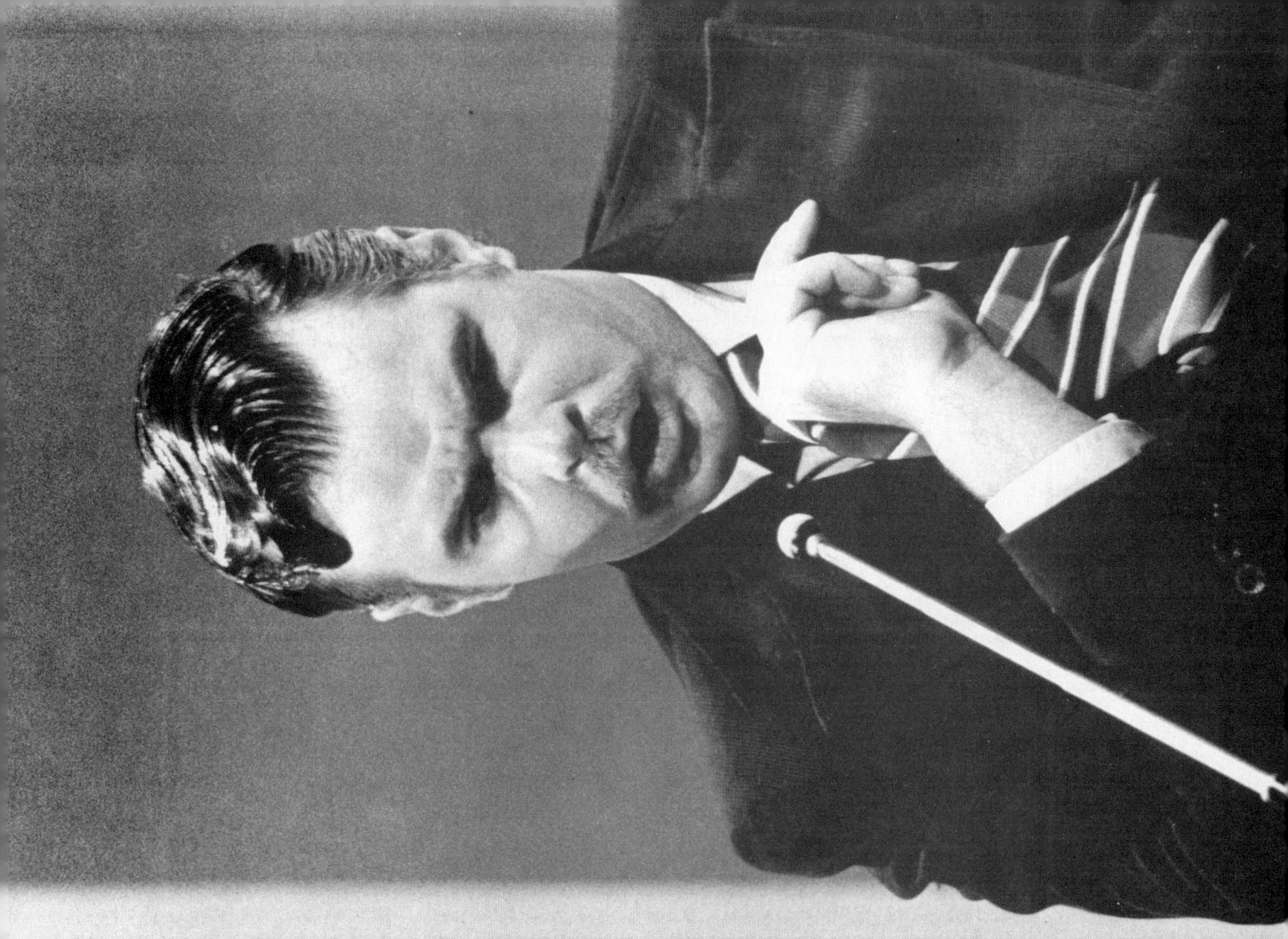

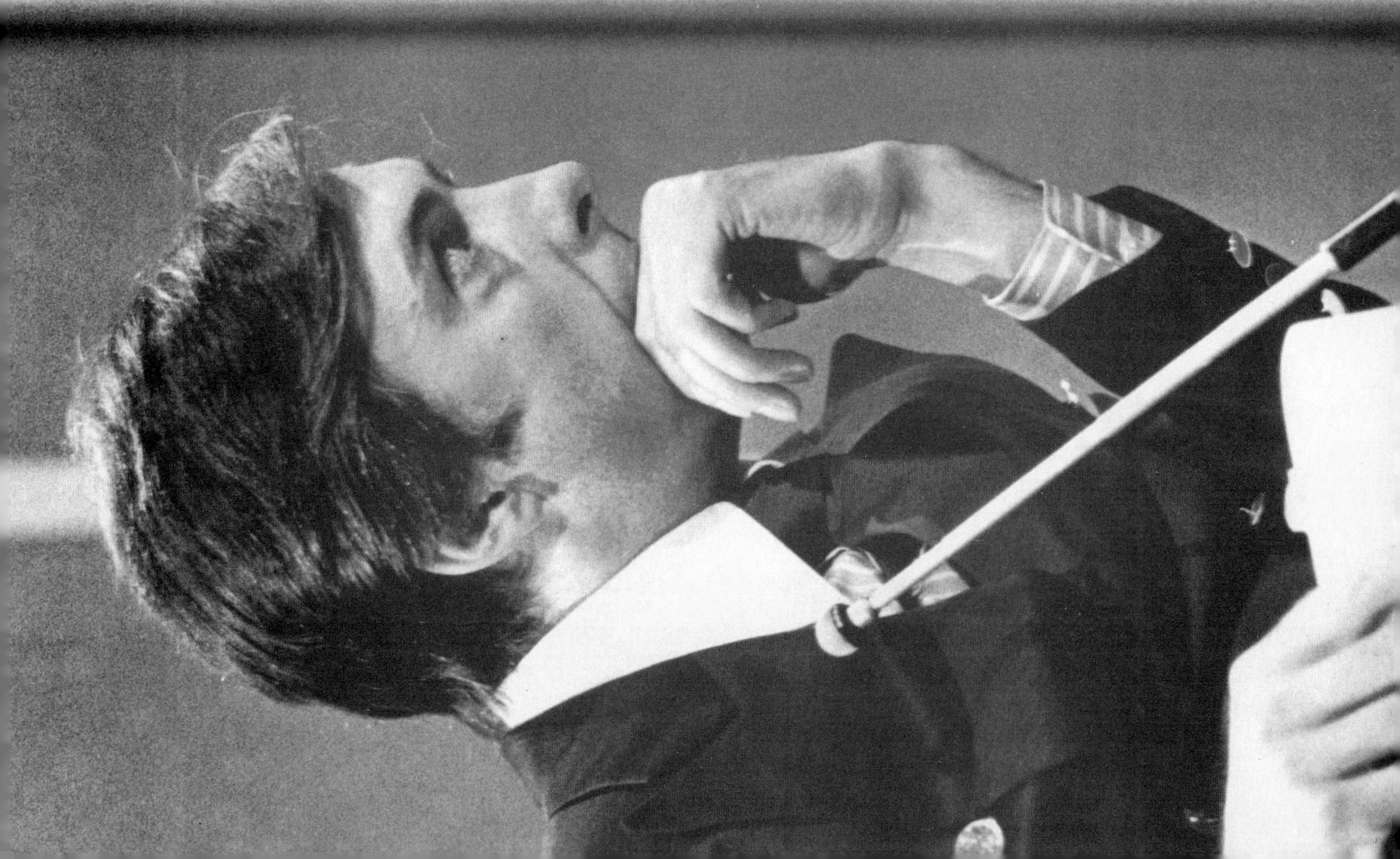

THE COMEDY

SELECTED SKETCHES

Weekend Update

This sketch is truly a SNL classic. From the first season to the present, this parody of television news has been an important segment. As a showcase of comedic talent for both writers and performers, WU's prodigious output of characters and personalities has been unequalled. Beginning with the launching of Chevy Chase's rise to stardom, WU has consistently entertained the audience.

Jane Curtin, solo initially, then with Dan Akroyd, followed Chevy in the anchor position, Later Bill Murray was at the news desk.

John Belushi's manic weatherman exploded on the WU set. Gilda Radner's Emily Litella gave Jane Curtin fits; Rosanne Rosannadana made her nauseous to the audiences delight.

WU gave Garrett Morris his one hit character, Chico Esquela. Don Novello's Father Guido Sarducci gained nationwide recognition.

WU did have its off time, though. Charles Rocket's tenure at the anchor desk in the 80-81 season is for the most part forgettable with the exception of Joe Piscopo's Saturday Night Sports. Later WU provided a showcase for Rich Hall, Dennis Miller, and Kevin Nealon.

Rosanne Rosannadana

Gilda Radner's Weekend Updates special news correspondent with a huge head of thick frizzy black hair, bulging eyes, and an ever-present wad of chewing gum in her mouth; whose rambling news pieces would inevitably transform into a grotesque description of some bodily function, or its similarity to some food. A viewer's letter to Rosanne would usually provide initial topic such as the unhealthy aspects of eating beef, leading to Rosanne's recollection of the time she quit eating red meat and ate only fish. She ate so much fish she thought "I was gonna die."Which in turn leads to her telling how she really did not like fish, especially oysters which feel like big phlegm balls in your mouth. By this point Jane Curtin as Weekend Update's very business-like anchorperson, jumps in to tell Rosanne that she was making everybody sick and had completely wandered from the topic. After being chastized by Jane, Rosanne would reply "Well Jane, it just goes to show you, its always something...."

followed by words of wisdom in the form of a song or poem written by one her relatives, Nanna Rosannadana, or Carlos Santana-Rosannadana.

Baba Wawa
Gilda Radner's imitation of Barbara Walters, exaggerating her lisp. "Not For Women Only" Baba interviews "Wiving Wegend Marwena Dietwich" (Marlene Dietrich) played by Madeleine Kahn, also with a severe lisp. Written with as many L's and R's as possible, their lisping makes it difficult for anyone to understand what they're talking about.

Nerds
A SNL fan favorite from the early years. Bill Murray and Gilda Radner as suburban American high school nerds, (Todd Di Lamuca and Lisa Loopner respectively) supported by Jane Curtin as the widowed Mrs. Loopner. Todd was dressed in the male nerd essentials; high-water pants with belt up to armpits with the ubiquitous and fully-loaded pocket-protector-pen-and-pencil holder in his shirt pocket. Lisa was characterized by her thick horn rimmed glasses (constantly sliding down her nose), a sweater draped off her hunched shoulders, and her mouth hanging wide open to allow for her labored asthmatic breathing. Todd and Lisa's physical appearance were as funny their witless repartee.

In nearly every sketch Todd would look down Lisa's shirt to see if there were "any new developments" and then offer his medical advice, "Better put some band-aids on those mosquito bites!" Lisa's responses typically were "That's so funny I forgot to laugh," or "The last time I heard that I fell off my dinosaur."

Classic "Nerd" Sketches include "The Nerds Christmas Pageant", "The Nerds Prom," and the sketch in which Dan Akroyd appears as a plumber and gives America's network TV audiences their first good look at construction-worker's buttocks cleavage.

The Bees
A recurring sketch on *SNL* in which the all cast members were dressed in bee costumes. One of the Bees first appearances placed in a maternity ward of a hospital, when a nurse bee enters to tell the new father "Its a Drone."

In a later Bees sketch, Belushi plays a waiter serving host Rob Reiner and his wife Penny Marshall. Shortly into the sketch Reiner breaks character and complains, "I was told 'no Bees' when I signed on to this—they're ruining the show!" to which Belushi replies ranting, "I'm sorry if you think we're ruining the show, Mr. Reiner. But, see, you don't understand— we didn't ask to be Bees. You see, you've got Norman Lear and a first-rate writing staff. But this is all they came up with for us. Do you think we like this? No, no, Mr. Reiner, we don't have any choice. You see, we're just like you were five years ago. Mr. Hollywood California Number One Big Shot! That's right—we're just a bunch of actors looking for a break, that's all! What do you want from us Mr.Star. What did you expect, the Sting?"

Another Bees sketch had the cast with Elliot Gould dressed as a gang of bandito Killer Bees swarming into America from the South.

The Bees became one of *SNL*'s first hit sketches. The only common thread the Bees sketches had was the costumes. Belushi and Akroyd actually performed their first manifestation of the Blues Brothers on *SNL* in the Bees outfits when they played "king Bee" together on the show.

The Coneheads

One of *SNL*'s most popular running sketches. Featuring Dan Akroyd, Jane Cutain and Loraine Newman as Beldar, Prymaat, and Connie Conehead, a family of aliens from the planet Remulak living unoticed in suburban America.

When Earthlings inquire about their origin, the Coneheads say they are from France. Their efforts to fit into the American lifestyle included their propensity to "consume mass quantities" of beer and potato chips.

Landshark

Chevy Chase dressed in a large foam rubber shark head. He goes to New York City women's apartments and tricks them into opening their door so he may devour them. In one, he intones "Candy-gram" in a mild business-like voice while the ominous music from the movie *Jaws* plays in the background.

Samurai

John Belushi as a Japanese Samurai warrior placed in the most unlikley scenarios. In the first appearance, with Richard Pryor, the two Samurai bell boys argue over who will bring guest bags up to a room. Pryor ends the argument by chopping the check-in counter in half with his sword.Belushi says, "I can dig where you're coming from."—the only words in English Belushi's samurai would ever say.

Other Samurai sketches included a disco spoof Samurai Night Fever, Samurai Deli, Samurai Tailor, Samurai Divorce Court, and Samurai Psychiatrist

Olympia Diner

John Belushi as Pete, the diner owner; Laraine as the waitress; Dan Akroyd as the cook; and Bill Murray as the counterman. This popular sketch became known for its refrains: "Cheeseburger Cheeseburger" and "No Coke... Pepsi!". In the Oympia Diner, the only thing you could order was cheeseburgers and Pepsi, even at breakfast

Nick the Lounge Singer

Bill Murray's trademark *SNL* character—a slimy, Ramada Inn-quality cocktail lounge piano entertainer whose act was always basically the same; lame renditions of mindless pop music. Nick appeared in a variety of settings to do his show, from a ski lodge to cheap roadside taverns to an Arctic army base.

Don't Look Back in Anger
A short black and white film by Tom Schiller in which John Belushi plays himself in old age and goes to the cemetary where all his fellow cast members from *SNL* have been laid to rest. He visits each grave and tells a bit about what each did after *SNL*:

Gilda had her own TV show in Canada for years;

Laraine is said to have murdered her husband then moved to California where she owned a pecan farm, and died of anerexia;

Jane-married a stockbroker, had two kids, and moved to upstate New York before dying of complications during cosmetic surgery;

Garrett worked in Black theatre for years, then died of a heroin overdose;

Bill lived the longest–38 years;

Chevy Died right after first movie with Goldie Hawn;

Dan died on his Harley, clocked at 175mph before the crash.

The film ends with Belushi saying *Saturday Night* show was the best experience of my life, and now they're all gone. I miss every one of 'em. Why me? Why did I lived so long? They're all dead. I'll tell you why . . . 'cause I'm a dancer!"

Uncle Roy
Played by frequent guest player Buck Henry. Uncle Roy was the babysitter for two young girls, played by Gilda Radner and Laraine Newman. Uncle Roy would play a variety of perverted games with the girls, including: Buried Treasure, when the girls would have to search for a secret buried treasure hidden in Uncle Roy's pants pockets; Horsey, in which he gave the girls rides on his back; Ruffy the Dog, when he was spanked by the girls for being bad; and the notorious Glass Bottom Boat game in which the girls dressed in their little dresses and panties and sat on the glass coffee table while uncle Roy watched from underneath

Mr. Bill
Created by Walter Williams. A *SNL* classic, these short animated lowbudget films featuring the Play-Doh doll Mr. Bill, who was invariably pulverized, torn apart, or smashed by the sinister team of Sluggo (another play-doh character) and Mr. Hands. "OH, NOOOO" was howled by Mr. Bill before his inevitable demise in each episode.

The Czech Brothers
Jorge and Yortuk Festrunk, two brothers who had escaped from Czechoslavkia to the United States, now live "to meet foxes". Their calling card became "We're two wild and crazy guys!" Played by Steve Martin and Dan Akroyd, they were easily identified by their tacky disco attire–tight polyester bell bottom pants and gaudy print polyester shirts unbuttoned to the navel with large medallions hang-

ing around their necks—and unique way of walking with knees deeply bent, shoulders slung back, and rocking back and forth, with fingers snapping.

The French Chef, Julia Childs
Dan Akroyd, as Julia Childs, starred solo in this hilariously bloody sketch. In it the French Chef prepares some complex recipe when she cuts herself. "I've cut the dickens out of my finger," Akroyd announces in Childs' shrill voice, as copious amounts of blood begin to spray from her wounded hand all over the kitchen counter. She tries, unsuccessfully, to administer first aid to herself to stop the flow of blood, begins to lose consciousness, then bleeds to death.

Mr Robinson's Neighborhood
Probably Eddie Murphy's most popular character. A parody of PBS's benevolent children's show, *Mr. Robert's Neighborhood*, Murphy plays a street-wise ghetto hustler hosting a childrens show from his ghetto apartment and teaching the boys and girls watching about the ways of ghetto life: illegitimate children, stealing, mugging, "scumbucket" landlords, and all.

The word of the day could range from "bastard", on the show when Mr. Robinson's old girlfriend leaves their illegitimate child in a basket at his door, to "ransom", when Mr. Robinson kidnaps someone's dog. Performed by Murphy with his face beaming an insincere smile into the camera, this sketch is probably most famous for Murphy's wide-eyed and puckered-lipped mug into the camera when the phone rings or there is a knock at the door, before he gently says "Who could that be boys and girls?" then bellows in the loudest and most intimidating voice he can muster "Who is it?"

Prose and Cons
Sketch satirizing Norman Mailer's relationship with convicted murdered/author Jack Henry Abbott featuring Eddie Murphy as convict/poet Tyrone Green reading one of his poems.
Dark and lonely on a summer night
Kill my landlord, kill my landlord
The watch dog barking
Do he bite?
Kill my landlord, Kill my landlord
Slip in his window
Break his neck
Then his house I start to wreck
Got no reason
What the heck?
Kill my landlord, kill my landlord
K-I-L-L my landlord.

Buckwheat
Eddie Murphy's impersonation of Buckwheat, of Little Rascals fame, as an adult. Though grown up, Buckwheat still has that high-flying electro-shock hairdo and cannot speak English intelligibly.

Murphy's Buckwheat was a huge show biz star. The first Buckwheat sketch to be aired was a spoof commercial for his new record album *Buckwheat Sing,* featuring his renditions of "New Nork, Ndew Nork" and "Fee Times a Mady"

Eventually Murphy's Buckwheat character was put to rest forever on a show which had running gag in it— the assassination of Buckwheat. This show satirized the TV Networks overblown but empty coverage of the assassination attempt of President Reagan with its constant repetition of the video tape of the shooting and a corporate sponsor of the coverage.

Velvet Jones
Eddie Murphy's slick-haired pimp peddling his career self-help book for female high school dropouts entitled "I Wanna Be A Ho."

Gumby
Eddie Murphy portrays Gumby, the green clay children's show character, as an ornery, over-the-hill, prima-donna Jewish show business personality from another era. Murphy's Gumby was always clutching a large cigar and shouting, "I'm Gumby, dammit!"

The premise of the Gumby sketches included Gumby as the writer/director of his own rise-to-stardom life story, Gumby's Christmas special, "Merry Christmas Dammit" with special guests the Don King family, an incestuous Donny and Marie Osmond, and Joe Piscopo's Frank Sinatra crooning the Flintstones and Woody Woodpecker songs.

Dion Dion
Eddie Murphy as the effeminate hairdresser who appeared on various sketches; as expert guest on "Hairem, Scarem", a talk show for people with hair salon horror stories; as a contestant on the game show spoof "What Would Frank Do?"; and in sketches with Blaire, another gay hairdresser (Joe Piscopo).

What Would Frank Do
A game show sketch in which the contestants must correctly guess what Frank Sinatra would do in various scenarios.

Frank goes to his favorite restaurant for dinner, his regular table is already occupied—What would Frank do?

Correct answer: *Frank would buy the restaurant.*

This sketch was created by some of the writers after getting tired of dealing with Joe Piscopo who would frequently reject doing material saying "Frank wouldn't do that."

Frank Sinatra
Joe Piscopo played Frank many times on *SNL*. Piscopo's Sinatra appeared in many unlikely scenarios, including singing the Flintstone's and Woody Woodpecker songs on the Gumby Christmas Special.

One of the most famous sketches was when he appeared with Eddie Murphy's Stevie Wonder to record a song together. Sitting at the

piano together Frank begins his rendition of Stevie Wonder's "Ebony and Ivory" with the following lyrics:
You are black
I am white
Life's an eskimo pie
Let's take a bite
That was groovy thinkin', Lincoln
When you set them free.

Doug and Wendy Whiner
Joe Piscopo and Robin Duke. The insufferable Whiners, Doug and Wendy, are perfect for each other, but a curse for the rest of humanity, with their whining voices and numerous health and medical problems. They push everyone to the breaking point, demanding and impossible to please. Whether its out to dinner for their anniversary or to studio 8-H to see *SNL,* they are never happy.

Ed Grimly
Martin Short's most famous character during from his one season on *SNL*. A spastic swivel-waisted urban geek, Grimly's most recognizable features were his greased back hair, parted on both sides of his head with the center pulled up into a strange formation that resembled a Hershey's chocolate Kiss. His catchphrase: "I must say," constant use of the word "decent", and worship of game show host Pat Sajak or Alan Tribeck were trademark characteristics.

Mr. Subliminal
Kevin Nealon appeared in his own sketches and as a commentator on Weekend Update. He would squeeze various "subliminal" messages—"you buy", "bring money", "talk dirty to me", "hot sex", "your place".

First seen in sketch with Leslie Nielson, they play two men from an advertising firm visiting a local bar working together on a subliminal advertising campaign. Nielson's character doesn't understand this subliminal advertising at all. Nealon plies his subliminal charms to get free drinks, money, and a wallet from the bartender, then picks up an attractive woman for "hot sex". Nielson, thinking he understands, tries to subliminally talk his way out of a parking ticket, resulting in his arrest.

Pumping Up with Hans and Franz
Dana Carvey and Kevin Nealon parody TV instructional fitness programs. They portray Arnold Schwarzenegger's cousins Hans and Franz, dressed in over-stuffed gray public school style sweatsuits with big leather weight-lifting belts, combat boots, and spikey crew-cut hairdos. The macho and pompous pair belittle everyone else on the planet except for themselves and Arnold. Their favorite insult is: "you are a flabby girly-man loser".

Although they claim, "We are not here to talk, We are here to pump (clap) you up," all they do is talk about themselves and perform their hilarious convulsive muscle flexing.

The Anal Retentive Chef
The Anal Retentive Fisherman
The Anal Retentive Carpenter
This series of sketches featured Phil Hartman as Gene, the anal retentive host of a variety of documentary how-to shows. In these sketches nothing actually ever gets done, because Gene is too preoccupied planning, cleaning, and putting utensils, equipment, or tools in their alphabetically designated place.

Wayne's World
This recurring sketch of a community access cable TV program run by heavy metal heads Wayne Campbell and his sidekick Garth Algar from Aurora Illinois is filled to the brim with key phrases. "Not", "Schwing!", "Party on!", "As if...", "Hurl!", "Excellent", "Sphincter", "...till monkeys fly out my butt", "Way.... No Way", "We're Not Worthy". Starring Michael Myers as Wayne and Dana Carvey as Garth, they host the show produced in the basement of Wayne's parents suburban home.

Sketches range from Letterman-like Top ten lists such as the Top Ten Babes of All Time to Wayne's World Oscar Picks to Special guests. Show guests include Aerosmith (by virtue of Garth's cousin being a roadie for the band), Wayne Gretzky, and Rick (Bruce Willis) the coolest guy in school on the show to "invent the new cool word for the school year—'Sphincter'". Chick Court is held on the show so that one their fellow high school students, Lisa Harwin (Debra Winger) may dispel rumors that she is a slut.

Highlights of the sketches are the brief pseudo-intellectual asides to the TV audience. One such was the explanation of their selection of Josephine Baker as one of the Top Ten Babe of All Time. Wayne's World also uses lots of cheap camera tricks—unnecessary zoom, switcher solo, extreme close-up, silent scream, and the like.

60 Minutes
This takeoff of CBS News' *60 Minutes* show is one of the best sketches of the '84-'85 season. It featured Harry Shearer as Mike Wallace, Christopher Guest and Billy Crystal as Herb and Al Minkman, owners of America's largest manufacturer of novelties, and Martin Short as Nathan Thurm, a corporate lawyer for a Hong Kong company making defective novelty products.

"Mike Wallace" does a typical *60 Minutes* investigative report on cheap imported novelty products, their health hazard to the public, and the detrimental effect on the economic viability of the American novelty manufacturing industry. He interviews the Minkman brothers who extoll the superior quality of their US made products, and fool Wallace with fake spilled coffee and dog-do.

They give Wallace a tour of the R&D facility where miniature squirting toilets and whoopie cushion are being tested. The Minkmans are funny, but the hightlight of this sketch is Short's defensive, chain-smoking, sweating lawyer Nathan Thurm. Thurm answers Wallace's questions with his own questions, accusations, or his favorite line, "I know that."

The exchange went something like this:
> Wallace: Mr Thurm let's be honest. We've seen your people working for pennies making defective items, which at best don't work, and don't provide hours of family fun, and at worst are creating serious injuries.
> Thurm: (pause): So what are saying?
> Wallace: That your boss, Mr. Lee, is in effect the Mr. Big of the pirate novelty business.
> Thurm: No he isn't. You're just saying that to get higher ratings on your TV show.
> Wallace: I wish I were, but, we saw your people making pirate Minkman schnazes.
> Thurm (shaking head no and looking nervousy into camera): I don't know what you are talking about. It so funny that you say that. They don't make schnazes, they make semiconductors for a very reputable computer company. What's wrong with that? (speaking faster) Is there something wrong with that? Why is that, suddenly, something wrong to do? I don't understand that. Why are you pointing the finger at other people all the time? Why don't you point the finger at yourself? Do a little more reading maybe. Less time in court. Maybe that would be effective for you.
> Wallace: Pardon me for saying this, but you seem defensive.
> Thurm (quickly): I'm not being defensive, you're the one who's being defensive. Why is it that the other person is always the one that's being defensive? Have you asked yourself that? Why don't you ask yourself that?.
> Wallace: This is an affidavit . . . .
> Thurm (cutting off Wallace): I know that!
> Wallace: Well let me finish. This is an affidavit from a women who's got severe nerve damage on her upper thighs from sitting on one of your defective whoopie cushions. Here read it.
> Thurm: You read it.
> Wallace: Well I have read it
> Thurm:. So why do I have to read it.
> Wallace: Well it does pertain to your company.
> Thurm: I know that. Why wouldn't I know that? It is my company. I'm quite aware of that. (looking towards camera) Is it me? It's him, right?!

Tippy Turltle
This cartoon sketch was the mid-Eighties *SNL* version of Mr. Bill. Although not very original, it was funny and totally lacking in redeeming qualities.

The central character, Tippy Turlte, is an absolute louse, drinking and smoking constantly. His forte was mean practical jokes such as writing "THIS IS A STICK-UP!!" on the back of a deposit slip at a bank and returning it to the pile of blank slips, to, as Tippy put it, "get some poor hammerhead I never met before into a whole big ugly mess of trouble." Tippy was pretty accurately summarized by the sketch's theme song: "First I'm gonna bother everybody I meet. Then I'll probably go home and get drunk."

Fernando
Billy Crystal's Latin sycophant talk show host became famous for his refrain: "You look mahvelous." Impeccably coiffed and dressed in his insigniaed blue blazer with wide-collared white shirt and ascot, Fernando would make insightful conversation with his guest. A typical comment was uttered when Ringo Starr appeared on Fernando's Hideaway: "Boy that Beatles thing really took off, didn't it."

I Hate When That Happens
Billy Crystal and Christopher Guest starred in this bizarre and masochistic recurring sketch. Crystal and Guest appear as co-workers in various jobs (construction workers, policemen, performers in a waterski show, etc.) and discuss the grotesque and painful things they do to themselves. such as poking knitting needles through their nipples, twirling them around, and letting them go to spin like the propellers on a B-29 bomber or taking twelve feet of barbed wire and shoving it up one nostril and out the other then tying it to a full grown mountain gorilla and shooting a starter's pistol. After describing their self-tortures, they say "Boy is that painful" or "I hate when that happens."

The Copy Machine Guy
Starring Rob Schneider as Rich, supported by Michael Myer as co-worker Tom, Kevin Nealon as gay co-worker Randy, and Phil Hartman and Victoria Jackson as Steve and Sandy. Rich is the self-appointed guardian of the copy machine. His only form of communication with his co-workers is the repeated mangling of their names. Steve becomes the Steve-ster, Steve-ola, Steve-meister; Randy turns into the Rand-O-nator, The Rand-ster.etc.

In one sketch, Drew (Jeremy Irons) is given a going away party. Rich gives Drew the manual to the Xerox Telecopier 7009 as his gift and babbles variations of Drew's name as he mourns his departure.

Sprockets
German talk show parody with a supercilious, sexually ambiguous, and deviant host, Dieter (Mike Myers), and his monkey Klaus. Dressed completely in black, Dieter parades a variety of bizarre guests through his show, including Grous Greck (played by Woody Harrelson), introduced as "avant-garde film maker and irritant-in-residence at the Bremen Gallery of Modern Art". Grous is on to plug his new counterculture theme park, Euro-Trash, built in response to Euro Disney, as a "celebration of all that is repellent and painful in European life".

Special features have included "Germany's Most Disturbing Home Videos" compiled by special guest Karl-Heinz Schalker (Kyle McLauchlin (Twin Peaks). Dieter usually cuts off his guest and ends the show with "Your story has become tiresome. Now is the time on

Sprockets where we dance" and he is joined by identically dressed men dancing mechanically to the show's Euro-techno-beat music.

The Sinatra Group
Phil Hartman as Frank, Sting as billy Idol, Jan Hooks as Sinead O'Connor, Michael Myers and Victoria Jackson as Steve and Edie Gormet, and Chris Rock as Luther Campbell of 2-Live Crew.

Deep Thoughts
By Jack Handy This off-beat segment of *SNL* consists of two incongruous elements; the tranquil New Age background music and peaceful background images of nature's beauty (an ocean sunset, or a mountain stream running through a meadow of wildflowers) and the bizarre messages scrolling across the screen:

To me, clowns aren't funny. In fact, they're kinda scary. I've wondered where this started, and I think it goes back to the time I went to the circus and a clown killed my dad.

Contrary to what most people say, the most dangerous animal in he world is not the lion or the tiger or the elephant. It's a shark riding on an elephant's back, just trampling and eating everything they see.

Laurie got offended when I used the word puke. But to me, that's what her dinner tasted like.

Pat
Julia Sweeney's androgynous character sketch. The running joke is that no one knows whether or not Pat is male or female. All the supporting characters lack the guts to ask the question directly, continually trying to uncover Pat's sex.

The Superfans
Chris Farley and Mike Myers sketch satirizing local news pre-game shows for major league sports teams.

Lothar of the Hill People
Mike Myers plays Lothar, leader of an early Middle Age tribe (Viking or Saxon, perhaps). Lothar and his male tribesmen complain about the faults and weaknesses of women, but the women rule their lives in spite of their male superiority.

Oh My God
Melanie Hutsell, Beth Cahill, and Siobhan Fallon play three virtually brainless sorority sisters who scream "Oh my God!" at nearly every insignificant event of their TV-watching, junk-food-eating, gossip-mongering college experience. They speak in that annoying Valley Girl accent—the same inflection on each syllable spoken.

Their entire existence revolves around their sorority, Tri-Delta. They answer their house phone with the hokey greeting "Delta Delta Delta can I help ya, help ya, help ya."

The Receptionist
David Spade plays the unflappable receptionist at Dick Clark's office. No matter how big or famous a visitor is, he or she is greeted with the same line—
"*And you aaare.....?*" "*And he would know you becaaause.....?*"
—forcing the celebrity visitor into the ego-deflating position of having to identify themself; something celebrities hate having to do.

President Bush
Since 1990 Dana Carvey's wickedly funny impersonation of President Bush has practically become the standard cold opening sketch for SNL. Exaggerating the President's broken syntax and repetitive mechanical gestures, Carvey's Bush seems to be insecure, pleading for the audience's approval, explaining why he is not responsible for any of our country's problems.

Carvey's Bush visits Noriega in prison and apologizes for busting him, then reminisces about what a great team they were. Finally Noriega talks a reluctant Bush into helping with a new plan to assassinate Daniel Ortega.

Another hilarious Carvey Bush sketch begins with the President talking about global warming and soon moving on to his glaucoma and his doctor-prescribed eye drops with THC. As he puts the drops in his eyes, he dribbles most of it on his face and into his mouth, lapping up as much as possible with his tongue. It finishes with the president singing, "Lucy's in the sky with diamonds."

THE LEXICOON

Certain words, phrases, and slogans were popularized by *Saturday Night Live* and became identified with the show. This lexicon has been an integral part of the show's success. The title of the show itself has become part of this lexicon as the phrase "Live from New York, its Saturday Night!" has been used to finish off nearly every one of the show's cold openings for the last seventeen years. This lexicon grew out of recurring characters and sketches created by the writers and performers which were embraced by the show's fans. These recurring characters, adored by fans, were what opened the door for mass audience appeal and success for the show.

•"We're two wild and crazy guys"

•"I'm Chevy Chase — and you're not."
Chevy's trademark opening line as Weekend Update's first anchor person. Chevy became SNL's first star.

•"Jane, you ignorant slut!"
Dan Akroyd's opening rebuttal to Jane Curtin in Weekend Update's issue debate feature *Point/Counterpoint*.

•"Nevermind."
Gilda Radner as the elderly and sweet but hard-of-hearing Miss Emily Litella whose editorial comments on WU were always finished early when Chevy Chase or Jane Curtin clarified Miss Litella's thoughts on such problems as "Too much violins on TV" or the repercussions of President Ford making Puerto Rico a steak.

•"I thought I was gonna die!"
•"It just goes to show ya, its always something, if its not one thing, its another!
Gilda Radner's Weekend Updates special news correspondent

•"Baseboll has been berry, berry good to me."
Garret Morris as WU sports reporter Chico Esquela.

•"You know darling, it is more important to look good than to feel good and darling you *look* mahvelous!

•"Isn't that special!"
Satan

•"We're here to pump-(Clap)-you up!" "Believe me now and hear me later." "Girlie Man",

•"Not", "Party on!" "As if...", "Hurl!", "Excellent", "Sphincter", "...till monkeys fly out my butt", "Way .....No Way", "Babe", "Babe-alonian", "licensed babe-tician", "Oscar time again" Schwing", "I'm starting to feel tingly down there", "Fished in", "We're not worthy!"
All key phrases popularized by Wayne's World, perhaps the sketch which has generated the most additions to the SNL Lexicon!

BORING, BUT NECESSARY ORDERING INFORMATION

Payment:
Use our new 800 # and pay with your credit card or send check or money order directly to our address. All payments must be made in U.S. funds and please do not send cash.

Shipping:
We offer several methods of shipment. Sometimes a book can be delayed if we are temporarily out of stock. You should note whether you prefer us to ship the book as soon as available, send you a merchandise credit good for other goodies, or send your money back immediately.

Normal Post Office: $3.75 for the first book and $1.50 for each additional book. These orders are filled as quickly as possible. Shipments normally take 5 to 10 days, but allow up to 12 weeks for delivery.

Special UPS 2 Day Blue Label Service or Priority Mail: Special service is available for desperate Couch Potatoes. These books are shipped within 24 hours of when we receive the order and normally take 2 to 3 three days to get to you. The cost is $10.00 for the first book and $4.00 each additional book.

Overnight Rush Service: $20.00 for the first book and $10.00 each additional book.

U.s. Priority Mail: $6.00 for the first book and $3.00.each additional book.

Canada And Mexico: $5.00 for the first book and $3.00 each additional book.

Foreign: $6.00 for the first book and $3.00 each additional book.

Please list alternatives when available and please state if you would like a refund or for us to backorder an item if it is not in stock.

COUCH POTATO INC.   5715 N. Balsam Rd   Las Vegas, NV 89130   (702)658-2090

Use Your Credit Card 24 HRS — Order toll Free From: **(800)444-2524** Ext 67

ORDER FORM

- ____ Trek Crew Book $9.95
- ____ Best Of Enterprise Incidents $9.95
- ____ Trek Fans Handbook $9.95
- ____ Trek: The Next Generation $14.95
- ____ The Man Who Created Star Trek: $12.95
- ____ 25th Anniversary Trek Tribute $14.95
- ____ History Of Trek $14.95
- ____ The Man Between The Ears $14.95
- ____ Trek: The Making Of The Movies $14.95
- ____ Trek: The Lost Years $12.95
- ____ Trek: The Unauthorized Next Generation $14.95
- ____ New Trek Encyclopedia $19.95
- ____ Making A Quantum Leap $14.95
- ____ The Unofficial Tale Of Beauty And The Beast $14.95
- ____ Complete Lost In Space $19.95
- ____ ..doctor Who Encyclopedia: Baker $19.95
- ____ Lost In Space Tribute Book $14.95
- ____ Lost In Space With Irwin Allen $14.95
- ____ Doctor Who: Baker Years $19.95
- ____ Doctor Who: Pertwee Years $19.95
- ____ Batmania Ii $14.95
- ____ The Green Hornet $14.95 ____ Special Edition $16.95
- ____ Number Six: The Prisoner Book $14.95
- ____ Gerry Anderson: Supermarionation $17.95
- ____ Addams Family Revealed $14.95
- ____ Bloodsucker: Vampires At The Movies $14.95
- ____ Dark Shadows Tribute $14.95
- ____ Monsterland Fear Book $14.95
- ____ The Films Of Elvis $14.95
- ____ The Woody Allen Encyclopedia $14.95
- ____ Paul Mccartney: 20 Years On His Own $9.95
- ____ Yesterday: My Life With The Beatles $14.95
- ____ Fab Films Of The Beatles $14.95
- ____ 40 Years At Night: The Tonight Show $14.95
- ____ Exposing Northern Exposure $14.95
- ____ The La Lawbook $14.95
- ____ Cheers: Where Everybody Knows Your Name $14.95
- ____ SNL! The World Of Saturday Night Live $14.95
- ____ The Rockford Phile $14.95
- ____ Encyclopedia Of Cartoon Superstars $14.95
- ____ How To Create Animation $14.95
- ____ How To Draw Art For Comic Books $14.95
- ____ King And Barker:an Illustrated Guide $14.95
- ____ King And Barker: An Illustrated Guide II $14.95

100% Satisfaction Guaranteed.

We value your support. You will receive a full refund as long as the copy of the book you are not happy with is received back by us in reasonable condition. No questions asked, except we would like to know how we failed you. Refunds and credits are given as soon as we receive back the item you do not want.

NAME:_____

STREET:_____

CITY:_____

STATE:_____

ZIP:_____

TOTAL:_____ SHIPPING_____

SEND TO: Couch Potato, Inc. 5715 N. Balsam Rd., Las Vegas, NV 89130